—BOOK TWO—

GUNNER'S REDEMPTION

USA TODAY BESTSELLING AUTHOR

HEATHER SLADE

GUNNER'S REDEMPTION
© 2018 Heather Slade

This book is a work of fiction. The names, characters, places and incidents are products of the writer's imagination or have been used fictitiously and are not to be construed as real. Any resemblance to persons, living or dead, actual events, locale or organizations is entirely coincidental.

Paperback:
979-8-88649-115-9

MORE FROM AUTHOR HEATHER SLADE

BUTLER RANCH
Kade's Worth
Brodie's Promise
Maddox's Truce
Naughton's Secret
Mercer's Vow
Kade's Return
Butler Ranch Christmas

WICKED WINEMAKERS
FIRST LABEL
Brix's Bid
Ridge's Release
Press' Passion
Zin's Sins
Tryst's Temptation

WICKED WINEMAKERS
SECOND LABEL
Beau's Beloved
Coming Soon:
Cru's Crush
Bones' Bliss
Snapper's Seduction
Kick's Kiss

ROARING FORK RANCH
Coming Soon:
Roaring Fork Wrangler
Roaring Fork Roughstock
Roaring Fork Rockstar
Roaring Fork Rooker
Roaring Fork Bridger

THE ROYAL AGENTS
OF MI6
Make Me Shiver
Drive Me Wilder
Feel My Pinch
Chase My Shadow
Find My Angel

K19 SECURITY
SOLUTIONS TEAM ONE
Razor's Edge
Gunner's Redemption
Mistletoe's Magic
Mantis' Desire
Dutch's Salvation

K19 SECURITY
SOLUTIONS TEAM TWO
Striker's Choice
Monk's Fire
Halo's Oath
Tackle's Honor
Onyx's Awakening

K19 SHADOW OPERATIONS
TEAM ONE
Code Name: Ranger
Code Name: Diesel
Code Name: Wasp
Code Name: Cowboy
Code Name: Mayhem

K19 ALLIED INTELLIGENCE
TEAM ONE
Code Name: Ares
Code Name: Cayman
Code Name: Poseidon
Code Name: Zeppelin
Code Name: Magnet

K19 ALLIED INTELLIGENCE
TEAM TWO
Coming Soon:
Code Name: Puck
Code Name: Michelangelo
Code Name: Typhon
Code Name: Hornet
Code Name: Reaper

PROTECTORS
UNDERCOVER
Undercover Agent
Undercover Emissary
Coming Soon:
Undercover Savior
Undercover Infidel
Undercover Assassin

THE INVINCIBLES
TEAM ONE
Decked
Edged
Grinded
Riled
Smoked

THE INVINCIBLES
TEAM TWO
Bucked
Irished
Sainted
Hammered
Ripped

THE UNSTOPPABLES
TEAM ONE
Furied
Merried

COWBOYS OF
CRESTED BUTTE
A Cowboy Falls
A Cowboy's Dance
A Cowboy's Kiss
A Cowboy Stays
A Cowboy Wins

Table of Contents

1

Gunner

My life was made up of a series of nightmares strung together like a broken strand of lights that my subconscious forced me to relive night after night after night, waking me up in a cold sweat.

My dreams used to vary, featuring one horrific reenactment after another of harrowing escapes, hostile gunfire, exploding IEDs, and other forms of death and destruction.

Now, the first thing I saw whenever I closed my eyes, was the woman I'd been forced to kill, staring at me.

"Paps, I thought you loved me," she said in every dream, even though she'd never actually uttered those words. They were only spoken in my nightmares when her eyes met mine at the very moment she realized I'd killed her.

Lena "Barbie" Hess had been under K19 Security Solution's protection since the day we opened for business. Prior to that, her detail had been the responsibility of an elite team comprised of active-duty service members and CIA agents, called the Special Activities Division of the agency's National Clandestine Service—otherwise known as NCS.

My best friend and teammate, Razor, had asked me once if I loved Lena. There'd been a brief moment in time when I saw the bright light of the woman she'd once been, before darkness reigned over her life. In an instant, she was gone again, unable to pull herself out of what I now knew was mental illness. If only I'd known how to help her then. Now, it was too late. She was dead—and I'd killed her.

"Do not do this, Lena. If you think I won't shoot, you're wrong," I'd shouted as her eyes darted between me and a man who was like my brother, a man she'd just shot, and who was on the ground—with his gun still pointed at her.

I watched her take a deep breath, close her eyes, and tighten her finger on the trigger. Before she could get the shot off, I fired first.

I ran toward her, catching her before her head hit the concrete. There was no question she was dead; I'd hit her square in the chest with a .45. No one could survive a shot like that.

"Goddammit," I'd cried, cursing her for forcing my hand.

As I'd watched Lena's lifeless body being taken away that day, I'd made two decisions.

First, that "Paps," the code name I'd been given by my special ops teammates, would be buried with her.

Second, I'd never allow myself to fall for any other woman again. My resolve had lasted less than a handful of hours, when the woman I was now risking my life to rescue, wound up in my bed.

Zaryana "Raketa" Ivashov had been undercover on the same op that resulted in Lena's death, initially posing as her nurse and caregiver after an accident had left Lena blind and amnesic.

When the operative was tasked with providing her safe passage to Moscow, Lena had thanked the woman the intelligence world knew as "the Rocket" by putting a bullet in her brain—or so she'd thought.

* * *

"Shit," I gasped when I saw Raketa's body lying in a pool of blood.

I ran forward and checked for a pulse, nodding at my teammates when I found one.

That she was still alive meant the bullet had either grazed her skull or was still lodged in her brain. If it was the latter, the chance she'd survive was slim. However, without immediate medical attention, it would be certain.

Raketa's eyes fluttered open when I whispered her name. She groaned and tried to sit up.

"Stay still," I told her, motioning for my teammates to go ahead.

As risky as it was, I called for backup. "Send a medic," I said into my radio mic.

"Who shot you?" I asked, trying to get her eyes to stay focused on mine.

"Lena," she groaned. "Go. Find her. She's…"

When she lost consciousness again, I closed my eyes and said a silent prayer, all the while keeping my finger on her still-active pulse.

I knew I had to leave her when the medics arrived, as hard as it was to go.

* * *

Later, I learned the shot had only grazed Raketa's scalp, resulting in enough bleeding that Lena believed she'd successfully offed the woman.

I didn't remember much about the night we'd spent together, except I knew we'd had sex until I finally passed out. Then, in the morning, she'd sneaked out while I was in the shower.

A few months passed before I heard from Raketa again, and then she wanted to make a deal. She told me she knew who had kidnapped the victims of my then-current op and where they were being held. In exchange for that information, she wanted my help with an op of her own—leaving the employ of United Russia, or in other words, defecting.

Agreeing to help her was what had landed me in the bowels of hell, otherwise known as Baku, Azerbaijan, trying to find where a Russian black market arms dealer was holding her prisoner and, more importantly, why.

2

Zary

Makar Petrov was a cold-hearted *sonuvabitch,* but I doubted he'd kill me. If he was going to, he would've done it by now.

If it weren't for Rauf "Topor" Evasov, I would've killed Petrov first, but instead, I'd ended up his captive.

I still cursed the emotional reaction I'd had when I saw Petrov put a gun to the head of a woman who shared my DNA. Letting my guard down, not pulling the trigger for fear I'd kill the woman rather than the man who was my target, was what had allowed Topor to knock me out and load me onto Petrov's plane.

The circumstances of my incarceration certainly weren't what most would consider a hardship. Instead of keeping me in a cold, dark room, Petrov had ensconced me in an apartment within his compound in Old City Baku. I'd been told I was free to come and go within its ancient walls, which dated back at least to the twelfth century, although some contended they were constructed as long ago as the seventh.

I could probably live out the rest of my life here. Petrov would keep me safe from United Russia, who'd put a price on my head of over a million dollars. However, there were two reasons I couldn't do that.

First, I'd never work in intelligence again, unless it was for Petrov, and then it would have to be done within the confines of the Old City because I wouldn't be let out of it in my lifetime, or his.

The other thing was, I'd never see Gunner Godet again. The man likely had no recollection of the last time we were together. It was the same day he'd saved my life, and I'd gone in search of him to offer my thanks.

* * *

"You shouldn't be here. What the fuck are you doing here?" Gunner scowled through a drunken haze when I found him sitting in the otherwise empty bar.

"Paps, you're—"

"Don't call me that," he barked.

"*Izvini,*" I muttered. "I know Lena was—"

Before I realized what was happening, Gunner stood and grasped my neck, holding it tightly enough that it was difficult for me to breathe, but not enough that he cut off my air supply entirely. If I wanted to, it would be easy for me to break free. Instead, I absorbed the pain flowing from his fingertips.

"Never say that name again either. Do you understand me?"

I couldn't nod or speak with his hand on my throat, but my eyes bored into his.

"Never," he spat again, this time releasing me.

I sat down at his table when he did, and lifted the half-empty bottle of vodka. "May I?"

He grabbed it from me, stood, and stalked over to the bar. When he returned, he slammed a glass on the table in front of me and poured.

I didn't wait for the toast that would typically be expected. I threw the shot back and poured myself another. This time I waited for him since his glass was still full.

I kept my hand clasped around the icy-cold vodka and my eyes focused on his.

"Leave," he said, throwing his shot back.

I shook my head and watched the only other person in the room, the bartender, follow the command and walk out.

Gunner inched closer, leaning forward enough that I could feel the heat of his breath.

"I want to be left the hell alone," he seethed.

"No." I'd been where he was too many times, but never because I'd killed someone I cared about.

"Then, I'll leave." Gunner stood, tucking the bottle of vodka in the crook of his arm. He swayed just slightly, but caught himself.

"No," I said again.

He slammed the bottle back on the table and grasped my neck, this time from the back.

"You saved my life," I whispered.

"You would've lived."

If Gunner moved closer, our lips would touch. Instead of waiting for him to do it, I kissed him.

"Fuck," he groaned as he wound his arm around my waist, pulled my body flush with his, and slid his tongue between my lips.

When I put my arms around his neck and pressed my breasts against his chest, Gunner stuck his knee between my legs.

"Take what you need, Rocket Girl," he taunted when I straddled his powerful thigh.

"Not here," I said as he moved his leg, backed me up against the wall, and put his hands beneath my bottom.

"Put your legs around me," he demanded.

When I did, he ground himself against me.

"Is this what you want?" he asked before bringing his lips to mine and kissing me in a way that no man ever had or ever would again.

* * *

When I'd gone looking for him that night, it was to thank him. Being with him, close enough to touch, had left me as breathless as it did thoughtless.

He'd ravished my body most of the night, but then I'd left without saying goodbye while he was in the shower. Part of me wished I'd stayed to see how he'd handle the morning after, but at the time, I hadn't been brave enough. What if he remembered the first time we'd met after he sobered up? Worse, what if he didn't?

Gunner Godet had haunted me since my early twenties. When we first came face-to-face, I should've killed him and the other American spy the KGB had tasked me with assassinating. I couldn't, though. My eyes met Gunner's and it was as though a bolt of lightning had struck me motionless. I'd lowered my gun and let the two men escape. If any of my *comrades* had witnessed what I'd done, I would've been executed on the spot.

I told myself that wanting to defect and leave the employ of United Russia had nothing to do with Gunner, but when I decided to finally do it, he was the one I'd contacted for help.

I'd had to bargain for his assistance, and even then, he'd reminded me over and over that he couldn't guarantee my safety.

Whether he could keep me safe or not, there wasn't another team in the world who could help me make the break like K19 could. Since they'd formed a tentative alliance with the current president of Russia's political party and intelligence organization, I had hoped K19 and UR might be able to make a deal to secure my defection.

But Petrov had stripped away my hope for freedom. In fact, now it was worse. While I may not be his hired gun, I was his prisoner.

Gunner would come for Petrov; his intention had always been to assassinate him, but that didn't mean he'd come for me.

3

Gunner

I'd been out of communication with the rest of the team searching for Makar Petrov for almost forty-eight hours, mainly because we weren't searching for the same person. My priority was finding Raketa Ivashov, and while I knew they were aware of it, it wasn't something the teams on the ground—Onyx and Alegria from K19, Striker, whoever the hell he was with currently, or the MI6 team, headed up by Shiv—and I ever discussed.

No one knew what I had planned, and I intended to keep it that way. Since even I didn't understand my connection to the Russian assassin, I couldn't very well explain it to my teammates.

Maybe it had been seeing her lying in a pool of blood and believing she was dead, or seeing a brief glimpse of her vulnerability when she came to me, asking for help, that hit me hard enough that I'd opened the doors of my heart the thinnest of cracks.

It took balls of steel for someone to even think they could walk away from an organization like United Russia. Doing it was a death wish. I admired the tenacity she'd exhibited when I told her as much.

I often wondered if Raketa remembered the first time we saw each other. We'd been on opposite sides of an op involving a CIA agent who was on the verge of being burned if my team didn't cross over the border from Kazakhstan into Russia to extract him.

I'd been in my mid-twenties, and while I now knew she was only two years younger than me, then she'd looked barely eighteen.

I'd never forget when our eyes first met. I'd come close to death that day—closer than I had up to that point in my career—and all because I'd hesitated. She could've shot me and the man I was assigned to extract, but she didn't. She'd lowered her gun enough that I knew if she did fire, it would hit the ground.

Her beauty had left me almost breathless. I knew from intelligence photos that Raketa's long, straight blonde hair hung past her waist when she left it loose. Piercing blue eyes coupled with the pallor of her skin were striking to the point of being heart-stopping. Raketa was thinner than I usually preferred a woman to be. How much thinner would she be now, after being in Petrov's clutches?

The fact that Petrov hadn't killed her was as troubling as it was a relief. What reason would he have to take a UR assassin hostage in the first place, particularly given she hadn't been a direct threat to him when she was captured? I couldn't come up with any answer that made sense.

My plan for today was to attempt entry into Baku's Old City. I'd dyed my usually reddish-blond hair black, put dark-brown contacts in to mask my green eyes, and the scruff of a beard I'd been letting grow longer was dyed the same color as my hair. Between that and my usual mostly black attire, I fit in well in a country that had as many Armenian citizens as Azerbaijani.

4

Zary

"He wants to see you," said Topor after unlocking and opening the door to the apartment without knocking. I was a prisoner; had I really expected privacy?

I stood and folded my arms, waiting for his next directive.

"Come," he barked, grabbing my arm when I didn't move quickly enough. If I wasn't certain that by doing so I'd end up dead, I would've taken the bastard down for manhandling me the way he was.

He led me down the same long corridor of rooms I'd passed the other time Petrov summoned me.

"Zaryana," Petrov said without raising his head when Topor pushed me into the room.

I hated his use of my given name. To me, it represented a time when I was too weak to stand up for myself—between the ages of eight and eighteen—before I'd become "Raketa" and had taken control of my own life.

Petrov looked up and waved my escort out of the room.

"Topor tells me you're not eating."

I responded with silence, the same way I had every other time he'd spoken to me. This time, though, I made the mistake of looking him in the eye.

"You may die today, little one, by trying my patience or starving yourself to death."

"I'll eat," I murmured.

"That's better."

"Why am I here?" I asked.

"You should have left well enough alone."

"I wasn't after you."

He raised an eyebrow.

"I wanted out of UR. K19 could help me do that, so I helped them. If *you'd* left well enough alone, neither of us would be here."

The truth was, until I came face-to-face with him in this very office, I hadn't believed the man really was Makar Petrov. I was very young the last time I saw him. I wouldn't have recognized him with or without the extensive plastic surgery he'd undergone.

"There are things…people…" he began.

I glared at him. "I cannot help you. You've made yourself a prisoner within these walls."

"There are people who will try very hard to get to me."

"The list of those who want you dead is endless."

Again, Petrov raised an eyebrow. "I don't care for your smart mouth."

"Are your prisoners often conversational?"

"You're here for your own protection."

"*Bullshit,*" I seethed. "I am not here to be protected. I am a prisoner."

"You may enjoy a great deal of freedom, Zaryana."

"Don't call me that, and as long as I'm here, I am not free."

"This is tiresome. You're home. Make the best of it."

"This is not my home. If it were, would your henchmen be permitted free access?"

"What are you referring to?"

"Topor…" I began, not sure what else to say.

"*Speak, girl,*" Petrov shouted at me.

"He doesn't knock."

Petrov scrunched his eyes together as though he was trying to figure out what I meant.

"I have not allowed him such privilege."

"Then, make him stop." God, I hated the sound of my own voice. The words that were coming out of my mouth were Zaryana's, not Raketa's. Raketa would never participate in a conversation of any kind with Makar Petrov. I turned my back to him.

"I could send you to United Russia. Let them deal with you."

I was stunned. Was he serious? "I'll be dead before I set foot on Russian soil."

Petrov shrugged. "The choice is yours."

"What choice?"

"Do as I say, or I'll let UR come and get you."

"What do you want?"

"Avarie and Aine."

I turned back around and stared at him, waiting for him to continue, refusing to ask what the hell that meant.

"I want my daughters brought here."

"No chance in hell," I answered, pained by his use of the word.

"Very well, then."

He called out for Topor to return me to the apartment.

Still not knowing whether Petrov would allow his henchman to punish me, or even kill me if I pushed him too far, I let him lead me back down the corridor without wrenching my arm out of his grasp.

As he dragged me back to my room, I heard the faint cry of another woman. I glanced at Topor, who showed no sign of hearing the same thing I had.

When the cry turned into words I could understand, I dug my heels in.

"Devochka moya," came the wail from a different corridor.

"Hurry up!" barked Topor, digging his fingers further into my flesh.

Only after he'd closed the door behind him and I'd locked it, did I rub my arm where he'd bruised my flesh.

The words I'd heard the woman cry were hauntingly familiar; something about them tugged at my heart. The hurt I felt was one I thought I'd buried when I was still a child.

An hour later, I heard another knock on the door and waited. Wouldn't whoever it was simply walk in like Topor always did? When I heard the second knock, I walked over.

Alegria stood just outside the threshold and motioned with her head for me to move closer.

"Dead zone," she explained, pointing to the ceiling just outside the threshold of the door. "We're setting up an extraction, but there's a complication," she continued, keeping her voice low.

I nodded, with my heart in my throat, almost afraid to believe that K19 had found me so quickly or that they planned to get me out. I didn't ask what the complication was; I assumed there were many.

"Another person. Not sure if she's a hostage," Alegria answered my unasked question.

"Who is she?"

The woman showed me a grainy image on her phone.

"Look familiar?" Alegria whispered.

I shook my head. It could be anyone. There weren't any features clear enough to discern.

She handed me a plate of food, and I reentered the apartment. As I closed the door behind me, I cursed myself for not asking who else was inside. There had to be at least two operatives, considering they'd found the areas where the cameras wouldn't pick them up.

5

Gunner

"Alegria is in. She's seen Raketa," Shiv said when I answered the MI6 agent's call.

"Where is she?" I asked, incredulous that they'd found her before I had, given I didn't think they'd spend time looking for her over Makar Petrov.

"They've got her locked up tight in a compound in the Old City."

"What's the plan for Petrov?"

"Gunner, we always protect our own first. You know this."

I was confused. Under what circumstances would Raketa be part of either of our teams? She was a UR assassin regardless of whether she planned to defect or not.

"Gunner?"

"I heard you."

"I'm waiting for instructions."

"From who?"

Shiv laughed. "You, you bloody bastard."

Normally, the plan would be immediate. Get in, get the hostage, get out.

"Let's meet at thirteen hundred," I answered.

"Roger that."

"I'll come to you."

"That'll be easier since we don't know your twenty."

That had been my plan. I didn't want anyone to know where I was or what I was doing. The meeting I'd requested would be to craft a plan for Petrov's assassination, not Raketa's extraction. I'd be handling that all on my own.

Striker and Shiv were head-to-head over something when I walked in.

"She's here," I heard Alegria say to them as she pointed to a rough drawing.

"Gunner," said Striker, the first to look up.

I looked more closely at what the two men were studying. "What is this?" I asked.

"An apartment."

"Where on the compound is Petrov exactly?"

"Unknown, for now, but we'll find him," Striker answered.

I studied the access points that they'd determined were weak.

"There's someone else here," said Alegria, pointing to a different area.

"Who?"

"I don't know."

"Do you have a theory?" I barked.

"Negative."

"Why does he have Raketa? What does he want with her?"

"I haven't been able to determine the reason, sir," she answered. "He did summon her earlier."

"And you know this how?" I demanded.

Alegria looked at Striker.

"Tell me you didn't plant anything."

"We don't intend to leave her in there long enough for anyone to find it," Shiv answered.

I got up from the table and looked out the window. "Five minutes is long enough for it to be discovered," I muttered.

"What's the plan, Gunner?" asked Shiv.

"I'm going in tonight."

"Where?"

I pointed to an area on the drawing. "I want *Armenian* transport arranged."

Shiv nodded. Everyone knew the Azerbaijanis and Armenians were mortal enemies. In the position we were in, only Armenians could be trusted not to hand us over to Petrov.

"To where?" he asked.

"London," I answered.

"It'll be taken care of."

I motioned for Shiv and Striker to follow me outside.

"Explain why you're going in to get Raketa before Petrov, and don't give me the shit about taking care of our own first," I demanded once we were out of earshot of the rest of the team.

"Getting her out makes the rest of our job easier."

I nodded. "What's the connection?" I asked.

"We haven't been able to draw a line between them," answered Striker. "Maybe she's somehow connected to the bodyguard that had been posing as his wife."

No one had suspected "Kelly McNamara" of being much more than Petrov's latest gold-digging wife when he'd been living his life as Conor McNamara. Although I did remember Razor saying the wife rankled him too.

When we went back inside, Striker suggested we check out the theory that Ivashov and Adrine Shah were somehow connected.

"I'll take a look," offered Onyx.

I nodded. I'd always liked the man who'd started out on our payroll solely as a pilot but had recently become a K19 partner. The thing I liked most about him was he only spoke when necessary. More people should be like that, in my opinion. However, another of our operatives, code name Monk, took it to an extreme.

I shook my head. What the hell was I doing, letting myself get distracted by anything that didn't directly involve getting Raketa out of Petrov's compound?

"We could delay twenty-four hours—"

"No," I snapped at Striker. "I'm getting her out of there tonight."

"Understood."

I turned to Shiv. "Once she's out, slit Petrov's damn throat."

We spent the rest of the afternoon reviewing the compound's security setup.

While Petrov may have been able to update some of it, the only way to get it airtight would be to tear it down and build again—something that would never be allowed in the Old City. Not that Petrov had the money to do much more than the bare minimum. The agency had made sure his assets were seized, but more importantly, they'd put a watch on his offshore accounts.

The man would soon be paralyzed financially, unless he had cash hidden, which was more of a probability than a possibility.

It was a simple in-and-out deal. Almost too easy. As much as I didn't want backup, I'd accepted it upon Shiv's insistence.

I checked the time. Four more minutes. In and out. Done. Raketa safe. Petrov dead. That was the plan.

6

Zary

I startled awake and sat up. The words I'd heard echoing in my head in my dream were the same ones I'd heard this afternoon. Worse, they'd been cried with the same voice I last heard when I was eight years old.

It suddenly became clear who the other captive was. She must have been held here since that fateful day twelve years ago when I was told both my parents were dead.

After seeing Alegria, I'd allowed myself to hope that, soon, I'd be free. Now I knew I couldn't leave until I figured out a way to take the other woman with me.

I stood and paced, trying for the third time to figure out a way to get the locked door of my apartment open. I'd known, when Petrov said I could "enjoy a great deal of freedom," he had not meant I could wander the corridors of the compound alone.

I heard a popping sound, and a moment later, and everything went black. With the moon hovering behind clouds, it was pitch-black.

I felt his breath before a hand slipped over my mouth and an arm encircled my waist.

"Shh," Gunner's voice whispered in my ear.

I tried to struggle but didn't make a sound. There was no question my apartment was being surveilled, and while the power may be out temporarily, I assumed the compound had backup generators that would kick on at any moment. I couldn't go with him, but I didn't want Gunner killed either, especially since he thought he was rescuing me.

As soon as I believed he was safely out of harm's way, I'd tell him I couldn't go with him.

"Ten feet," I heard him whisper into the mic in his earpiece. When we'd covered that distance, another door flew open. Just as he placed me on the seat of the waiting SUV and climbed in behind me, I heard the gunfire of those who had followed, but not quickly enough to stop us.

Four things happened simultaneously: Gunner pulled the SUV's door closed. The man in the passenger seat yelled, "Go!" The driver put the vehicle in gear and sped away. And my heart sank. I had no choice but to go with them now, at least temporarily. Instead of figuring out a way to get out of Petrov's compound without getting killed, now I had to figure out a way to get back in.

I grasped the door handle with one hand and the seat with the other as the vehicle careened through the narrow cobblestone streets of Old City.

Gunner and I made brief eye contact but didn't speak. Instead, I listened as he rattled off instructions to the driver.

It appeared that the plan they had prior to my extraction had changed. Or Gunner was changing it as we went. From what I could glean, we would be traveling north to Georgia and then west into Armenia. The driver seemed to think they could cross directly from Azerbaijan into our final destination, but Gunner disagreed.

He hadn't asked, but if he had, I would've concurred with his assessment. While we might be permitted to cross the border into Armenia, it would be at far greater risk than if we went through Georgia first. However, if we tried to cross over the border and were detained,

I'd have a better chance of getting away from the K19 team and back to Baku.

We were just outside the gates of Old City when two other SUVs came at us from either direction. Gunner grabbed my arm and pulled me from the vehicle we were in, to the SUV that appeared on our left. When the back passenger door opened, we slid inside.

"Good to see you, Raketa," said a man I never would've predicted would be a willing participant in my extraction—Striker Ellis, former CIA lead operative.

Alegria, in the front passenger seat, nodded.

Gunner sat closer to me than he'd been in the previous vehicle, enough so that I could hear him breathe. I couldn't explain why, but it soothed me. He turned and caught me studying him.

Our eyes met, and it was all I could do to not lean forward and kiss him. The only thing stopping me was the likelihood he'd push me away.

When I shifted and my arm brushed up against his, he flinched, just slightly, but didn't move it.

"*Izvini,*" I whispered, moving mine away.

"I've received the flight plan," Alegria reported.

"Where's Shiv?" Gunner asked.

"Meeting us in Alat."

"Petrov?"

"No sign of him."

"Fuck."

"We're a little less than three hundred kilometers from Ganja," Striker told him.

Gunner nodded again, but not enough that either of the two people in the front seats could've seen the slight motion of his head.

Out of the corner of my eye, I looked down at his arm, close enough that if I only moved a few centimeters, I'd be able to touch him again.

7

Gunner

In her sleep, Raketa rested her body against mine and her head on my shoulder, softly snoring. I turned my head so my lips were close enough to brush her forehead, but pulled away when I glanced up and met Striker's gaze in the rearview mirror.

I sighed and looked out at the darkness. In less than twelve hours, we'd be in London. I hadn't decided yet where Raketa or I would go from there.

Alegria turned in her seat and looked first at Raketa and then at me.

"The other person…"

I shook my head.

"I have a photo," she continued, disregarding the fact that I'd, in essence, told her not to.

Rather than answering, I glared at her.

Striker briefly turned his head. "Drop it for now, Mondreau," he murmured. "Get some rest, man," he added, looking over his shoulder at me.

I groaned inwardly, wondering what the hell my partners and I had been thinking by adding the two operatives sitting in front of me to our permanent team.

Get some rest? Had Striker actually said those words to me? If Razor were here, he'd be laughing so hard he wouldn't be able to speak. Doc, too. Mercer might find it funny, but I figured I'd kept our youngest founding partner intimidated enough, over the last couple of years, that he'd never laugh out loud.

Not to mention that Alegria had completely ignored me when I made it clear I didn't want her to continue asking questions about the other person being held captive by Petrov.

Once I knew what the plan was for Raketa, I would call a meeting of the original four partners and reinforce some of our ground rules.

While the newbies were technically "partners," they each held a minor share of the company. Doc, Razor, Mercer, and I still owned seventy-five percent of K19. The remaining twenty-five percent had been equally divided between Striker Ellis, Onyx Yáñez, Alegria Mondreau, Monk Perrin, and Dutch Miller.

We'd offered a spot to Mantis, but he'd turned us down. I wasn't sure what to make of that, but it wasn't any of my business.

There had been talk, mainly from Razor, about offering a partnership to Shiver Whittaker, but since he was next in line to run MI6, we decided to put that idea on the back burner.

The only other person I'd heard mentioned as a possible new partner was Raketa. Bringing her on as a contracted operative was one thing. That, I might be in favor of, but I'd never agree to offering her a partnership.

She stirred, murmuring something unintelligible in what sounded more like Azeri than her native Russian.

I knew that in her line of work, mastering not only languages but dialects too, was a necessary core skill. Perhaps she'd decided honing the language of Azerbaijan would be beneficial while being held captive by Petrov.

To my relief, we were getting close to Alat, which meant we'd soon be transferring from Striker's escort to Shiv's. It wasn't that I doubted the CIA agent's ability to handle our current situation; it was simply that I'd feel more confident with Shiver any day of the week.

Marquess Thornton "Shiver" Whittaker was one of the best operatives in the world. He and I went way back to one of my first missions for the NCS.

Right out of training, I was as green as they came. Doc and Shiv were both leads on that first mission, which meant I couldn't screw up too badly without either of my commanders cleaning up after me. I ended up learning a great deal from both men on that op.

It was Shiv's stealth that had impressed me the most. I'd studied, emulated, and finally asked Shiv if he'd consider training me. He'd agreed, and we'd been friends since.

In the world we operated in, I was second only to Shiver in my ability to get in and get out of almost any situation without anyone ever knowing I was there.

"Where are we?" Raketa asked, sitting up and moving away from me.

"Almost to our rendezvous point," I told her.

"Change of plans," said Striker from the front seat.

I tensed.

"What's wrong?" she whispered.

"Why?" I asked Striker.

"Something about a plane." The man smiled in the rearview mirror.

"Sonuvabitch," I muttered.

"This is a good thing, Gunner," Striker added.

"It's just a prop jet, but it'll get you out of Azerbaijan faster," reported Alegria.

"Where's Shiv?" I asked.

"Meeting you, asshole. Do you not appreciate—"

"Watch it," I warned.

Striker was used to ordering the K19 team around, not that any of us had ever paid attention to him. Now, though, things were entirely different. Striker no longer worked for the CIA; he worked for K19, and I had no intention of putting up with shit from him.

There was a clause written into the K19 partnership agreement stating that any of the new partners could essentially be forced out by a unanimous vote of the founding four. The leaving partner would be compensated, of course, but it allowed us a means to get rid of anyone we collectively deemed wasn't "working out."

No matter which partner came to the other three with an issue, it would be respected and dealt with. We didn't do this kind of work with someone we couldn't stand to be around or who didn't follow orders.

8

Zary

English wasn't my first language, but I knew what a prop jet was, and the plane I was looking at bore no resemblance to that type of aircraft. However, a plane of any kind seriously thwarted my plan to get back to Baku.

Looking at the jet as we exited the SUV, I guessed it belonged to K19. How Shiver had managed to get it to the private airfield was anyone's guess. However, MI6 had friends in places United Russia and even the CIA never would.

"Thanks," I heard Gunner mumble.

"Safe travels," Striker said as I passed by him. When he leaned forward to kiss my cheek, it was all I could do to stop myself from taking a step back. It was a friendly gesture and should be taken as such. I just wasn't used to public displays of affection of any kind.

I remembered being hugged, even cuddled, before my parents died. After that, I hadn't been shown another sign of affection by an adult.

Gunner stayed behind me as I followed Alegria up the steps to the plane.

"Mantis?" I heard her say, and watched as the two tentatively greeted each other. I witnessed the look that passed between them, and their body language, and guessed that something had gone on with the two operatives at some point in the not-so-distant past.

"Who's piloting?" Gunner asked, stepping inside the aircraft, behind me.

"I am," answered both Mantis and Alegria.

It was amusing, at least to me, but neither laughed. In fact, they squared off and glared at each other.

"Mantis is," said Shiv, coming up to the cockpit from the back of the plane.

"Alegria, you'll fly the second leg to London."

London? It would be next to impossible to get back into Azerbaijan if we made it all the way to the UK.

"Have a seat," Gunner said, ushering me through the galley.

I looked left and right, wishing he'd just choose a seat for me.

"Wait," he said, walking around me. "Follow me."

He went all the way to the back of the plane and opened a door.

"Get some rest," he said, putting his hand on the small of my back and leading me into a cabin that had a bed, two chairs, and a table. "Stateroom," he explained. "There are two."

I sat on the edge of the bed and looked into Gunner's eyes. Had he felt the current of electricity that passed between us at his simple touch?

"I'll be back to check on you later." He walked out the door.

I rolled to my side and closed my eyes. Gunner was right about me needing rest. I'd never felt this level of exhaustion.

The cabin door opened, and I shot upright. I had no idea how much time had passed since Gunner had left me to sleep.

"Settle down," he said, locking the door after he came inside.

I moved to the edge of the bed when Gunner sat in the chair.

"It's time for us to talk, Rocket Girl. What's the connection between you and Petrov?" he asked.

"There is no connection."

"Bullshit. Try again and tell me the truth this time."

I shook my head. The less I said, the harder it would be for him to pick up on my lies.

"Why did he take you to Azerbaijan?"

"I don't know."

Gunner rested his arms on his legs and leaned in closer. I waited for him to ask another question, but he didn't. He just stared at me.

We could sit right where we were for the rest of the flight, but no matter what he said or did, there'd be no way I'd divulge my connection to Petrov, to him or anyone else.

"Who's the other person being held captive at the compound?"

I did my best not to react to the question I'd antici-pated. "I don't know."

"What did Petrov want from you?"

"I don't know."

"You need to understand something, *devochka moya.* This is going to go one of two ways. Either you start telling me the truth, or once this plane lands, you're on your own."

When I looked away, trying to hide the tears that threatened with his use of the haunting endearment, he stood and walked out.

9

Gunner

I sat in the seat across from Shiver and opened the window shade. There was nothing to see, given what we were flying over was as desolate as Death Valley.

"Anything?" Shiv asked.

I shook my head.

"Once we land, we'll do a proper interrogation."

I looked into Shiv's eyes and saw amusement. "You're an asshole."

"And you just told me everything I need to know. How long has it been going on?"

"There isn't anything going on."

"Don't lie to me, you bloody bastard."

"You wanna tell me you never kept another MI6 agent warm on a particularly long and lonely op?"

Shiv grinned. "You know I have, and so does Doc."

"Fatale was above your pay grade."

"Fair point, well made. Although it wasn't for lack of trying on my part."

Merrigan "Fatale" Shaw was a former MI6, now married to Kade "Doc" Butler, and the managing partner of K19. The woman had been one of the best in the business, but semi-retired after she and Doc got married. Now they had a baby boy, and her husband behaved like she was the first woman in the history of the universe to give birth.

"I'll interrogate her," I told Shiv.

"You'll have plenty of time to."

"What's that mean?"

"The two of you are going dark until we find Petrov and see this mission through to the end."

"Back up. I am *not* going underground with Ivashov."

"You are."

I studied Shiv, trying to determine how serious he was.

"Where?"

"You'll be under MI6 protection."

That could be just about anywhere, other than the US, since there, we wouldn't need it. "You didn't answer my question."

"There's a safe house in the Cotswolds where I think the two of you would be very comfortable."

"I'm not a bodyguard."

Shiver raised a brow.

"I'm no longer offering those services. Onyx can take this assignment."

"What assignment?" asked Raketa, coming out of the stateroom.

"We're taking you to a safe house outside of London."

"No."

Raketa's response was so abrupt, I raised my head and our eyes met. "The hit United Russia has—"

"I've decided to return to Moscow."

I scrunched my eyes. "What are you talking about?"

Raketa raised her chin and squared her shoulders. "My words were clear."

"They'll kill you," I muttered, still studying her for any sign of what this might really be about.

"I have something they want. They will not kill me."

I stood. "What?" I asked, taking a step forward so I was directly in front of her.

"That is not your concern."

"I risked my life to get you out of Baku. You're not going to turn right around and walk in front of a firing squad."

Raketa put one hand on her hip and then lowered it as though she was about to argue my point but changed her mind.

"You assumed I wanted to leave the Old City."

I was ready to throttle her. What the fuck was this about? I spun around to get Shiv's take, but the man had left the main cabin. I turned back around and got closer still, so I was right in her face.

"Explain yourself," I seethed.

Raketa tried to take a step back, but there was a seat directly behind her.

"You came to me, asking for help," I said, still incredulous that the tack she'd decided to take was to return to Moscow, not that I believed that's what she was really going to do.

Even as close as I was, leaving her little room to look anywhere but at me, she refused to meet my eyes.

I grasped her arm and pulled her in the direction of the stateroom. She tried to wrench free, but I tightened my grasp, led her into the room, and locked the door behind me.

"One more chance, Rocket Girl. Tell me what this is about."

Raketa shook her head and remained silent.

"You'll tell me eventually," I said, walking out of the room and locking the door behind me.

"What the hell?" Shiv asked when I came back into the main cabin.

"You heard her. She's going back to Russia."

"Do you believe her?"

"Not even a little."

"What is this really about, Gunner?"

"My guess is her behavior has something to do with the person who is still being held by Petrov."

"But she won't give her up?"

"Negative."

"I need to know what happened between the two of you."

"Why?"

Shiv folded his arms but didn't answer.

"We were together the same night I killed Lena."

He nodded his head slowly, his eyes boring into mine as though he was trying to read my mind.

"But you have feelings for her."

It wasn't a question, not that I would've answered if it had been. How I felt about anyone or anything was no one's business. Did I care about Raketa? Obviously, to a certain extent, but beyond that, even I didn't know.

There was something that stirred in me every time I saw her, and got worse if she was near. I wanted her like I'd never wanted another woman.

Part of me wished I weren't so drunk the night we'd spent together, so I could remember more—more than how it had felt to sink deep inside her. I hated that the other events of the day had marred me finally being naked and alone with a woman I so often caught myself fantasizing about.

Raketa was planning something, and like I'd just said to Shiver, my guess was it related to the person Alegria had told us about at the compound.

Maybe if I could figure out Raketa's connection to Petrov, I could also determine who that person was.

No theory I'd come up with thus far made any sense. When Petrov was reported killed and disappeared from the face of the earth, believed to be at the bottom of the Caspian Sea, Raketa was a child. He'd reappeared in the States as Conor McNamara, married multiple times, and fathered two twin girls. There was no intelligence indicating that Raketa had ever worked for him or been associated with McNamara in any way.

Onyx was unable to make a connection between her and any of the people working for Petrov either, including the bodyguard who had been posing as his latest wife.

There had to be a reason why Petrov had abducted her from our last op, but it seemed that until Raketa told me what that was, it would remain a mystery. For now, she remained locked in the stateroom, which was laughable given we were on an airplane. It wasn't as though she could decide to walk away.

"That's quite a conversation you're having with yourself," said Shiv, still studying me.

I shook my head, stood, walked to the back of the plane, and put my key into the outer lock of the door. I didn't bother to open it; Raketa would know what I'd done and could come out if she chose to, although I predicted I wouldn't see her again until I either joined her or the plane landed.

"We've been cleared to fly directly to London," said Alegria from the cockpit.

I nodded. It would be harder for Raketa to stage an escape once we were on UK soil, but harder still if we traveled all the way to the US.

"I'll go underground with her, but not in the Cotswolds," I said to Shiv.

"Where, then?"

"The East Coast."

"Be specific, Gunner," said Shiv, smirking.

I walked away without answering because Shiv knew damn well where I was headed with Raketa.

I was taking her to a place almost no one knew existed. Doc, Razor, and Mercer did, but they were more than business partners; they were my best friends. Shiver knew about it too, but only because I'd needed the kind of help that only the MI6 agent could give me.

Raketa would be the next person to see the compound I'd spent the last couple of years constructing for my retirement.

10

Zary

I hated the tone of Gunner's voice as much as I loved it, especially when he called me Rocket Girl.

He was angry, and he had every right to be, but that didn't mean I could risk telling him the reason I wanted to return to Baku, or even that I intended to.

This was an op I'd handle on my own because if it failed, I'd never be able to forgive anyone who had been a part of it.

Once, he'd gone, there was no way I could fall asleep, regardless of how much I needed the rest.

Gunner would be relentless; I knew this. I had to craft a story more plausible than my intention to return to Moscow, but my brain wouldn't play along, and it was because I was mentally and physically exhausted.

Having Gunner so close didn't help. He'd had this effect since the first moment my eyes met his.

There was nothing soft about the man—every inch was rock-solid. At five feet, ten inches and in near-perfect physical condition myself, there weren't many men who made me feel petite, but Gunner did. It wasn't just his height—he had to be at least six feet, five inches—it was the girth of his torso as well as that of his extremities.

I'd heard stories from other Russian agents, detailing what he was capable of when it came to hand-to-hand combat. He could snap a man's neck without breaking a sweat and hurl someone weighing three times as much as I did through the air like a rag doll.

I knew he wasn't much older than me, maybe two or three years, but the life he'd led was etched on his face. The scowl he wore was ever-present, intimidating even his colleagues.

I'd seen his compassion, though. When he held me in his arms the day we both believed I was dying, his eyes had softened as had his voice.

"Rocket Girl," he'd murmured, holding me close to him.

As dangerous as the situation we were in had been, he still radioed for a medic, something I couldn't say I would've done if our situations were reversed.

I hadn't fallen in love with him that day, nor had my fantasies about him changed all that much. He was the main reason I'd accepted the assignment to escort the woman who'd try to murder me that very day, to Moscow.

The minute I'd heard the K19 team was on the woman's detail, I'd immediately accepted. That Gunner and I were on opposites sides of the op hadn't mattered. All I'd wanted was to be near him.

If I was being honest, he was the main reason I'd decided to leave Russia permanently, essentially signing my own death warrant. Once he'd agreed to help me, I knew he'd keep me safe. Just like, somewhere in the back of my mind, I'd known he'd come for me in Baku.

If he'd arrived twenty-four hours earlier, before I heard the wail of the woman who haunted my dreams, I would've gladly followed him to the ends of the earth, even if it had meant I simply worked by his side. That would've been enough, no matter how much my body craved more.

I'd known he was drunk the night we spent together, just like I'd known he wouldn't remember making love to me. Later, when we slept, just resting my head on his chest and feeling his powerful arms encircle me had given me a sense of peace unlike any I'd ever known.

What would Gunner do once the plane landed? Would he hand me off to one of the other K19 operatives? If I somehow managed to escape and returned to Baku, would he forgive me for putting his life at risk only for me to return to the place from which he'd rescued me?

It wasn't as though I had a choice. If the woman whose cries I heard was who I thought she was, I'd never be able to rest until I got her away from Makar Petrov.

I startled when Gunner came through the cabin door, just like I had earlier. I sat up, brought my knees to my chest, and clasped my arms around them.

"We'll be landing in London soon. We won't be leaving the plane."

"Why not?"

"Because London isn't our final destination."

I waited for him to divulge more information, finally realizing he had no intention of doing so.

"Are you taking me to the States?" I asked, feeling sick to my stomach.

Gunner nodded. "Unless you want to brief me on what your real plans are."

"I told you I am returning to Moscow."

"And I told you I know that isn't the truth."

"United Russia will negotiate my release," I said, refusing to look at him.

"They'll kill you, and you know it. And don't bother telling me that you have something they want. If that were the case, you would've told me that weeks ago when you asked me to help you defect."

Gunner sat in the chair by the bed and leaned forward, resting his elbows on his knees like he had earlier.

"Shiver suggested we let MI6 interrogate you."

I almost smiled. I knew Gunner would never allow that. If anyone interrogated me, it would be him or someone else from K19. Even then, it certainly wouldn't be traditional. He had other ways of getting information out of me, and we both knew it.

"Who will be my handler?"

Gunner smirked. "Me."

"My apologies, Zaryana," Gunner said as he cuffed my hands and blindfolded me. Neither bothered me as much as his use of my given name.

Rather than leading me off the plane, Gunner carried me.

"This isn't necessary," I muttered.

He didn't respond other than to tighten his grasp.

Navigating the exit stairs with me in his arms wasn't difficult for someone with Gunner's strength. His breathing didn't become labored nor did he shift my position until he deposited me in the back seat of a vehicle and fastened the seat belt around me.

"Thanks, boys," I heard him say before he closed the door behind me, and the car sped away. Only a few hours ago, he'd told me he would be my handler. Why had that changed?

I waited for the other occupants in the car to speak to give me some clue as to who they were, but neither did.

Resting my head against the window, I wondered if I'd seen the last of Gunner Godet. My heart hurt thinking I had.

We couldn't have been on the road more than two hours when the vehicle we were traveling in came to an abrupt stop and the driver cut the engine.

As I'd anticipated, the back door opened and a man helped me out. It wasn't Gunner, but whoever it was had a similar physique. They still hadn't spoken, which I knew was intentional, maybe even Gunner's orders. He was pissed, which meant he would do everything in his power to throw me off my game.

We'd walked a few feet when I heard a door open and felt a whoosh of cold air hit my face.

The man took my arm and led me inside, backing me against what felt like the edge of a bed. I sat down and waited while he unlocked the cuffs on my wrists.

By the time I shook the tingling out of my hands and arms and removed my blindfold, he was gone, the door shut and locked behind him.

The room didn't look any different than any other bedroom in any other safe house I'd ever been in. The windows were boarded over, and the lock on the door was a deadbolt.

I stood and stretched my arms over my head. There was no point in attempting to get out of here. It would be wasted energy. Soon enough someone would come for me; I only hoped it would be Gunner.

The place was clean, and I could smell the sheets on the bed were freshly laundered. On the dresser I saw a bowl of fruit, various cheeses, bread, and a carafe of ice water. Another door opened to a lavatory. They'd certainly made concessions for my comfort, although not as lavishly as Petrov had.

I shook thoughts of him away. What I needed to focus on was crafting a plan to do what I wished Gunner had done in the first place—kill the *sonuvabitch.*

After having a few pieces of cheese and some of the bread and fruit, along with several glasses of water, I struggled to keep my eyes open. I lay down on the bed, knowing sleep was inevitable, only then did it dawn on me why. The bastards had drugged me.

11

Gunner

There were several arrangements I needed to make before taking Raketa to my island.

I'd asked Mantis to secure the smaller of K19's planes so he didn't have to take her there by the same boat that would deliver our provisions. Once Mantis dropped us off, there would be no way for us to leave other than if I summoned someone to ferry us to the mainland. The island itself was impenetrable. Both Shiver and I had ensured it was a veritable fortress.

I'd likely thrown Raketa off by depositing her with Dutch and Onyx at the airport, but most of what I needed to arrange required phone calls I didn't want her to hear.

There were two things I had to accomplish while we were underground. First, I wanted to find out what her connection to Petrov was. Once Shiv succeeded in assassinating the evil *sonuvabitch*, I had to be certain there would be no repercussions from or for Raketa.

Second, I had to find out why she wanted me to believe she intended to return to Moscow and United Russia's employ.

"Hey, Raze," I said when my teammate answered the phone on the first ring.

"Wonderin' when you'd surface."

"I won't be up for air very long."

"Heard you got Raketa."

"Roger that, but she doesn't seem too happy about it."

Razor laughed. "You are an ornery bastard."

"I need your help."

"Name it."

I knew that would be my friend's response. It didn't matter what either of us needed or wanted; the answer would always be yes.

"Rocket Girl's history begins at age eighteen. I need to know who she was before that."

"Roger that."

"Thanks, man. I'll be back in touch when I can."

Razor didn't ask where I was headed as I knew he wouldn't.

"You want me to send a smoke signal when I figure it out?"

"Affirmative."

My response told Razor everything he needed to know. I'd just confirmed I was taking Raketa to Indian Springs Island.

"She's out," Onyx reported.

"Roger that," I said. "The plane is ready. I'll meet you there."

I had a very short window of opportunity if I wanted to get Raketa to the island before she came to. Once we were there, she'd have no means to leave. The closest land was a sixteen-mile swim.

I had no intention of manipulating her to get her to talk. I wanted Raketa to tell me the truth because she wanted to. That meant she had to trust me enough to open up, something her training had ingrained so deeply in her to never do. Breaking through those walls was going to take time.

I climbed into the small plane and put on the headphones Mantis handed me.

"There's a landing strip on the opposite side of the island," I told him, pointing to the map.

Mantis gave me a thumbs-up before pointing to where the SUV had just parked.

Rather than waiting for Onyx to bring Raketa to the plane, I jumped out and carried her myself.

"Thanks, boys," I said, motioning for Onyx and Dutch to head out.

The flight plan Mantis had filed would carry them just so far. Once they got close to the island, the small aircraft would intentionally lose contact with radar, land, and be stored in a well-hidden hangar. Mantis would be picked up by the supply boat and transported north into Maryland where he would be met by CIA agents who would take him to headquarters.

As much as I disliked Striker, I had to give the guy props for delivering as much as he had on this op. He no longer worked for the agency—he was a K19 partner now—but he'd been able to secure support from his former employer that even Doc wouldn't have been able to negotiate.

It wasn't just getting Raketa to come clean with me that I was concerned about. The threat against her from United Russia was very real. The last I'd heard, the bounty on her head had been raised to five mil. Doc was working hard to strike a deal with the modern-day equivalent of the KGB, but so far nothing he'd offered was equal in value to how much they wanted Raketa dead.

UR wasn't her only threat, either. There was a reason Petrov had taken her in the first place. If it had been for the money the Russians were offering, she would've been dead a long time ago. There had to be another reason.

I turned around and studied Raketa's sleeping form. Her beauty never failed to take my breath away or stir the kind of desire in me that no other woman ever had. We had chemistry. That much had been evident since the first time we saw each other and every time since.

In the last few months, the other three founding partners of K19 had met and married women that each of them, at one time or another, had professed to be their soulmate. I'd never believed in the notion, nor the other crap people in love spouted off about.

Each time I heard one of them go on about the love of their life, I couldn't help but inwardly call bullshit.

Mercer had been the first to tumble. He'd fallen for Quinn Butler who, as it turned out, was Doc's daughter. Until recently, no one had known she was, not even Doc. For sure anyway.

The day Mercer told me that he was giving up his partnership, retiring from the work we did, I was incredulous. I couldn't fathom why the kid would throw away his career and the money being a K19 partner pulled in just for a woman.

Doc was next when he announced his marriage, closely followed by his retirement. That hadn't surprised me. Doc had just returned from a harrowing two years being held prisoner by a Russian faction that United Russia wanted annihilated far more than they wanted Raketa's head on a platter. Doc's wife, Merrigan, had been the one who rescued him along with UR's help. Which was why now, Doc was taking the lead in negotiating for Raketa's life.

It wasn't until Razor met Ava McNamara that I began to believe in someone finding their one true love. Razor was as anti-bullshit as I was, and if there was anyone I would've predicted would die a sexually sated bachelor, it would've been Tabon "Razor" Sharp. But my buddy had fallen hard and fast for Ava, refusing to accept anything less from her than spending the rest of their lives together.

Razor had been on life support—close to death— but I knew he fought his way back for Ava.

When she came and found me sitting in the chapel, praying that God would spare my best friend's life, and told me that Razor was going to be okay, I'd closed my eyes and laughed, thinking that next time I wouldn't be so quick to call bullshit on things I'd never admit to—like the idea that maybe Raketa was more to me than a woman I wanted to have sex with. Maybe the inexplicably insane level of attraction I felt when I was with her could one day grow into something deeper.

I groaned at my own train of thought. I knew better than to think the kind of happiness that my teammates were experiencing would ever come to me. I'd learned that the day I'd killed Lena Hess. While I hadn't loved her in the same way Mercer, Doc, or Razor loved their wives, the pain I felt when she died was the worst I'd ever known, until a few weeks later when my father died.

"Everything okay, boss?" asked Mantis.

I nodded and looked out the window of the plane down at the deep blue waters of the Atlantic Ocean, wishing that Lena's memory had nothing to do with Raketa, because every time I found myself thinking this way, it always ended with how I'd killed her the same day I saved Raketa's life.

I closed my eyes momentarily and shook my head, trying to shake her ghost. Lena was hardly the first, nor would she be the last, person I was forced to kill. There'd been too many to count, first with special forces when I was a Marine, and then when I became part of the CIA's National Clandestine Service, and finally with K19.

Ridding the world of bad guys was what we did, and it wasn't something I ever allowed myself to think about long enough to have regrets. But with Lena, it had been personal, and her death had cut deeper than the rest combined.

I heard Raketa moan. Fearing she was coming to, I climbed to the back seat and shifted her so I could hold her in my arms. If she woke and reacted, I didn't want her to go after Mantis who was flying the plane.

Within moments, it became clear that she was having a nightmare. I couldn't decipher the words she said in her sleep, but for the second time, it sounded as though she was speaking Azeri instead of Russian.

"Getting ready to land," said Mantis.

I got Raketa strapped in, climbed back into the front, and secured my own seat belt. I looked ahead and saw the outline of my beloved island.

It had taken time, but I'd finally amassed enough money that I could build the house on it that I'd always dreamed of. It wasn't big, not like the house my mother and father had built when my dad retired from active duty, but it was big enough for me.

When I initially drew up the plans, I'd only intended to have two bedrooms. Razor had convinced me that was short-sighted.

"You might have a family one day, or at the very least, a former operative who wants to live here too," he'd said.

"You aren't welcome, and me having a family is an equally ridiculous notion."

"Better resale value if it has at least four."

Not that I ever intended to sell it, but Razor had made a good point. If something happened to me, my mother and sister might not want to hang on to a house on an otherwise uninhabited piece of land in the middle of the Chesapeake Bay.

My father had acquired the island from the Marine Corps while he was still a two-star general and was responsible for determining which land holdings that branch of the military should prudently hold on to and which should be divested.

If my father had tried to buy the island from the Marines now, even for a price that was fair, there'd probably be a congressional investigation into whether he'd unethically exploited his position.

In those days, the Marines didn't think twice about selling it to him. Doing so meant they didn't have to go to the trouble of finding another buyer.

A familiar feeling of pride engulfed my chest, knowing how happy my father would be knowing that I intended to retire here.

The only part of what I was feeling that confused me was how anxious I was for Raketa to see it.

Mantis landed the plane effortlessly and helped bring our gear to the waiting four-wheel-drive vehicle while I carried Raketa into the house.

When I laid her on the bed, she opened her eyes.

"Am I dreaming?" she asked.

I sat on the edge of the mattress. "If you are and I'm in it, it's not a dream, sweetheart; it's a nightmare."

Raketa closed her eyes and then reopened them. "I wondered if I'd see you again."

"Why?"

"I thought you handed me off."

I shook my head. "Soon you may wish I had."

"Not soon. I already wish you had. Why the fuck did you have to drug me?"

"I'm sorry about that. Truly. There were reasons…"

"Right. There are always reasons, particularly if you don't want your *subject* to know where you're taking her."

"It isn't like that."

"Right," she said again, sitting up and resting on her elbows. "Do you intend to torture me?"

"Depends on how you define it."

"Anything that involves pain."

"Physical or mental?"

"Both."

"Then, yeah, probably."

12

Zary

When I opened my eyes, the sun was shining, which meant I'd gone back to sleep after my brief conversation with Gunner and slept through the night.

I looked around the sparsely furnished room and thought about the things he'd said. Our conversation had ended far too quickly, with him telling me to get some rest and that we'd talk more in the morning.

I stood, stretched the stiffness out of my limbs, and peered out the window. I could see Gunner outside, doing a workout, no doubt positioned so he could see if I tried to leave the house.

I watched him for several minutes, marveling at how brutal his training regimen was.

I'd never pushed my body physically as much as I had when I was with him on the one and only op where we were on the same side, and I loved the way he'd challenged me.

Gunner could outdistance me in everything, but he'd never made me feel inferior, or as though he considered me weaker because I was a woman. It was more that he looked at us proportionately. He knew what he was able to do based on his weight, size, and strength. From that perspective, he'd pushed me to what he believed I should be capable of doing.

It was during that op that I'd offered my help in exchange for K19 securing my freedom from United Russia. It was also the op when Petrov's henchman, Topor, had caught me in the split second I was distracted by the woman Petrov held at gunpoint.

I closed my eyes at the memory. If none of that had happened, I'd never have heard the voice of the woman whose words I'd never forget. Somehow I had to get back to Baku and rescue her.

13

Gunner

I had no real plan for today, other than exorcising the last few weeks of inactivity out of my extremities. My body was used to being pushed, and when it wasn't, my age seemed to manifest itself in my joints and muscles.

Very few considered thirty-two old, except those younger than thirty-one. However, the life I'd led, the missions I'd undertaken, the days, weeks, and months I'd spent in hellholes like Afghanistan had aged me prematurely. Only pushing like I was this morning would eventually make me feel more like myself.

I caught a glimpse of Raketa's form in the window, but looked away without acknowledging seeing her there. She was watching me, likely wondering where we were and what would come next for her.

No doubt she was crafting what she thought would be a compelling story, intending somehow to convince me that she truly did want to return to Moscow.

We both knew she'd never set foot there again. If she did, even if Doc managed to strike a deal with UR, they'd kill her. They might still kill her anyway.

I picked up one of the tractor tires I'd had delivered to the island, hoisting it over my head before hurling it in the direction of the mark I'd set earlier. It fell short, but I'd soon meet it and move it farther away.

"Rocket Girl," I said, nodding when I saw Raketa standing outside the front door.

She smirked and gave me a half-hearted wave before taking several steps forward and looking first in front of her and then to the left and to the right, noticing water on all three sides.

"I'm guessing the view from the back of the house is similar."

I nodded. "You'd have to walk quite a distance, but eventually it would be."

"Will you tell me where we are?"

"There isn't any reason for you not to know."

Raketa folded her arms.

"Indian Springs Island." The concession wouldn't make any difference.

"Off the coast of?"

"Not important."

"Miles to the mainland?"

"Also not important."

"Is this your house?"

I nodded as she walked toward me.

"It looks like you."

I raised a brow and waited for her to continue.

"Sparse to the point of being cold. No sign of distinguished personality."

"Distinguishable?"

She scowled. "You know what I meant."

I smiled. She'd described my reputation accurately. That didn't mean she had any idea what I was really like. Few did. In fact, I could count the number of people who knew me well on one hand. My parents, my sister, Razor, and Doc. Even Mercer didn't truly know me.

"I see no need for frivolity," I countered.

"Friv what?"

I smiled again. "Extra stuff."

"It reminds me of Russia. Everything is gray."

"I found Russia to be quite beautiful."

"Perhaps you are colorblind."

I stepped closer to her. "I can see the difference between the color of your eyes and mine."

Raketa looked away, toward the water. "Why did you bring me here?"

I sat on the edge of the tractor tire. There were many reasons I'd brought her here. To keep her safe. To find out what her connection to Petrov was. To get her to stop lying to me. But those weren't the only reasons. There was one more that I had a hard time admitting even to myself.

"What's your connection to Petrov?" I asked instead of answering.

"There is no connection."

"Who is the woman still being held at his compound?"

There it was. I'd only caught a glimpse, but it was enough for me to see the flash of pain in her eyes.

"Who is she to you, Rocket Girl?"

"I've told you, I don't know."

I stood and picked up the tire, hoisted it over my head, and hurled it toward the mark. This time I met it.

I walked over and moved the stick another twenty feet and then sat back on the edge of the tire.

With the humidity and my physical exertion, my shirt was soaked all the way through. I reached behind me with one hand and pulled it over my head, tossing it on the ground near where I kept a cooler of water. I took a long drink and then wiped my mouth with the back of my hand.

My eyes met Raketa's, and I no longer saw pain in them. Instead, I saw heat.

14

Zary

There were many forms of torture; I had my own arsenal I'd used to get...*information.* However, the form Gunner was using wasn't intentional. Or was it?

There he stood, sweat glistening from a body almost too perfect to be anything but sculpted from stone, wearing nothing but workout shorts and shoes. It was all I could do not to run at him, knock him on the ground, and trail my tongue over the hard outline of his every muscle.

Instead, I went back into the house and stomped in the direction of the bedroom he'd deposited me in the night before.

I could hear his footfalls and prayed he wouldn't open the door I'd slammed shut.

When he didn't, my disappointment far outweighed my relief.

I looked in the closet, shocked to find clothes that weren't my own, but close enough to what I usually traveled with that they could've been. I found the same when I opened the drawers to the dresser.

"Who do these belong to?" I demanded when I stalked out to the kitchen with a few pieces of clothing in my hand.

"You," he answered without looking up at me.

"Why?"

This time he looked, raised an eyebrow, but didn't answer.

"I need a shower."

Gunner pointed toward the hallway. "Second door on the right."

I stalked back into the bedroom, rummaged through the clothes he'd provided, and then opened the door he'd indicated.

"This isn't a lavatory," I said, coming back into the hallway.

"Keep going."

I turned to go farther down the hallway.

"Into the room," I heard him say.

"What?"

Gunner walked over to me and opened the door I'd initially gone through. He stepped aside and motioned for me to go around him.

"This is your bedroom."

"And if you go through that doorway, you'll be in my bathroom."

"Don't you have another?"

Gunner shook his head and closed the door behind him, leaving me standing alone in a room that was vastly different than the rest of what I'd seen of the house.

Instead of the cool and neutral tones that were used in the bedroom I'd slept in, this one was done in rich dark brown and black. I never would've predicted it of him, but now that I was seeing it, the decor suited Gunner perfectly.

The wall the headboard of the bed rested against was covered with rough wood, with an outlined map of the globe etched into it. A ledge ran the entire distance of the wall where photos and other trinkets of memorabilia sat. Another of the walls was covered with rough and old-looking brick. There was a fireplace, holding several wood logs, built into the center of it.

It was the stuff sitting on the ledge that threw me the most. I never would've expected Gunner to be at all sentimental. The fact that he was, was almost shocking and, for some reason, made me sad.

Photos, trinkets, even memories, had never been a part of my life. I was an orphan, or had always believed myself to be.

When my parents died, I was sent to Moscow, alone, and had been met by a stern man who smelled horribly and didn't understand Azeri, the only language I spoke at the time.

He'd driven me to a "home" that housed both girls and boys, orphans like I was.

I'd lived there until I turned seventeen, when another man came to the home and took me along with seven other girls.

I remembered being one of the two in our group of eight who hadn't wept in fear, and thus, hadn't incurred the wrath of the man who came for us. Instead, I'd stayed quiet, hoping to make myself seem as small and insignificant as possible. When that hadn't worked, the only other girl who hadn't wept with the others, got between me and the man who likely would've raped me. She'd taken a beating, but spared me, who had been far smaller than her.

From that day on, that girl became my protector. We'd learned that the eight of us had been chosen because of our "better-than-average looks," in order to train us to work for Russian intelligence.

That woman and I had risen further than the others, eventually becoming assassins. She had been the one who'd first called me Raketa—the rocket. In turn, I'd called her Losha, for she was strong as a horse but could run like the wind.

I'd never bothered to remember the names of the other six girls, or even those of the men who'd trained me. There were other agents I knew and worked with, but given I preferred to work alone, I'd never established relationships with any of them either.

The hardest part about the night I spent with Gunner was that he hadn't given any indication that he realized I'd been a virgin.

He was the only man I'd ever been interested in having sex with, and the fact that he'd been my only and didn't realize it, hurt worse than I wished it did.

I shook away the self-pity and ventured farther, gasping when I walked into the bathroom.

One wall of the room was brick like in the bedroom and also had a wood-burning fireplace built into it. There was a section of the room that jutted out and had three walls of glass. A huge round soaking tub sat in the middle.

To the right of the door I'd entered through, there was another area separated from the main room by a partial wall that was almost as tall as I was. Behind the wall were two sinks that sat on top of the same rough wood that had been used in the bedroom, along with another door behind which I found a bidet.

If I had a bathroom like this, I wouldn't need a second one either.

What I didn't see was a shower. I walked over to the tub. Maybe this was my only option, and if so, it hardly afforded any privacy.

I looked for a tap to turn on the water and, instead, found an elaborate control panel on the outside edge of the porcelain. Studying it, I saw it had an option for a rain shower. I pressed the button and a circle of water, almost the same circumference as the tub itself, streamed from the ceiling. I stuck out my hand to find that it was already the perfect temperature.

Curious, I turned off the shower and pressed another button. Water streamed from the inside edge of the tub, and it was also the perfect temperature.

Torn between the two options, I decided to shower first, and then soak in the bath.

The luxuriousness of Gunner's bathroom was as surprising as what sat on the shelf in his bedroom. If I'd ever seen a photo of a space like this, I would've guessed that it belonged to a sheik, a king, or someone else as ridiculously wealthy.

I peered out the window before I climbed in the tub, but Gunner wasn't where I'd seen him before. I knew he'd gone outside; I'd heard the door close and then only silence.

As the water fell on my body, I closed my eyes and imagined that Gunner was here with me. I ran my hands over my body like I remembered him doing. I almost reached out my hand to steady myself, but then remembered I was surrounded by windows. Instead, I turned off the shower, turned on the bath, and sat down.

I had to stop thinking about being with Gunner and figure out how to get away from him. We were obviously on an island with no immediately visible way to get off. We'd gotten on, there had to be a way off; I just needed to figure out what it was and how to do it before Gunner realized I was gone.

What other option did I have? I couldn't tell him why I really wanted to leave, about my connection to Petrov, or to the woman being held captive on his compound. I couldn't tell anyone. The risk was too great.

15

I heard the water turn on, and then off, and then on again. Raketa must be playing with the controls of my combination bath and shower.

The house had two other bathrooms, but I'd sent her into mine for the simple reason that I wanted to show it off to her. Now, I was regretting it.

I was torn. If I went outside and continued my workout, I'd be able to see her through the bathroom windows that had never needed to be covered; there weren't any other inhabitants on the island.

My other option was to join her. That was, by far, the most tempting. While my memory of our night together was foggy, if I closed my eyes, I could remember how her skin felt against mine, how tight she was around me, and hear her soft whimpers of pleasure. Having her in the house that I'd had built to be my home, was almost too much of a temptation.

I was after information that would ultimately protect her more than anyone else. I'd never be able to live with myself if she believed I'd seduced her to get her to tell me what I wanted to know. That was a line I'd never cross, and while that wouldn't be the reason I longed to feel her naked in my arms, she would think it was.

In the end, I did neither. I went outside, but strode away from the house and through the forest that led to the other side of the island.

"I'm in trouble," I said out loud to no one but the trees. I thought about calling Razor, but wouldn't that make me the ultimate pussy?

My phone vibrated, and in an incredible stroke of coincidence, I saw that my best friend was calling.

"Hey, Raze," I answered.

"How you holdin' up, Romeo?" Razor laughed.

I thought about telling him he was full of shit. "Not well," I said instead.

"I've been where you are, and I couldn't be happier that I never have to go back."

I proceeded to tell him what I'd been thinking right before he called.

"Did you ever worry about Ava thinking it was just the op?"

"To be honest, I don't remember. I've welcomed the selective amnesia that prevents me from thinking about my life before she was in it. Although I do remember us arguing an awful lot. Wait, that isn't right. I remember her being mad at me. I doubt I ever had the balls to argue back."

"I remember. Every so often you grew a pair."

Razor laughed. "Listen, if you really want my advice, I'd say not to fight it. If the feelings you're having for her are that strong, then set your old grumpy, ornery self aside and do what your heart is telling you to."

"My *heart*? Seriously? What the fuck, Raze?"

"I can't help it. We're all rainbows and sunshine over here on the West Coast."

"Sunshine? In Oregon? Now I know you're lying."

I heard my friend take a deep breath.

"Why'd you call?" I asked.

"I have a theory I want to run by you."

If the tractor tire had been sitting in front of me, I could have thrown it two or three times the distance I had earlier. That's how angry I was.

I wasn't mad at Razor. It was my friend's theory that had me tied up in knots. If he was right, then I knew whatever relationship I might've thought possible with Raketa would never happen. Just like Lena.

However, this was worse. Lena had been mentally deranged. Raketa was flat-out lying to me about her true motives. I went so far as to wonder if, by having her here, my life was at risk.

I walked back toward the house and continued the workout I'd begun earlier, only this time with a vigor driven by my temper.

16

Zary

I sat up and saw Gunner stalk back to the tire he'd been hurling earlier. He looked angry, almost enraged. What could've happened for him to look as though he wanted to rip the rubber in two?

I waited to see if he'd look my way, but gave up after several minutes, emptied the tub, climbed out, and got dressed.

Instead of going outside, I went back into the room I'd slept in and sat on the bed. Maybe he was like this all the time. How would I know? We'd spent so little time together I really knew nothing about him, as much as it often felt the opposite.

Had I spun the fantasy of him so intricately that now I had to reconcile it with the man who was outside, punishing his body?

I peered through the window again, like I had when I first woke up, and saw him stalking toward the front door. Not knowing what to do, I stayed where I was and waited. Within moments, he stormed through the bedroom door.

"What is your connection to Petrov?" he bellowed, coming close enough that I thought he might grab me.

"There is no connection," I murmured.

"Bullshit. Quit fucking lying to me. Who is he to you?"

I stood my ground and looked him in the eye.

Gunner grasped the back of my neck and leaned in closer so our noses were almost touching.

"Who…is…he…to…you?" he spat, not lowering his voice even though I was right in front of him.

"He is no one to me."

"Let me rephrase, then. Who was he to you?"

I closed my eyes. He knew, or at least he sounded like he did, and he wanted me to admit it. I never would allow the words he wanted to hear to cross my lips.

"No one," I whispered.

Gunner raised his arm, but I knew he wouldn't strike me. He ran one hand through his hair while the other held tight to the back of my neck.

"Last warning. Tell me the truth," he barked.

Last warning, and then what? Would he leave and let someone else take over, someone who would interrogate me in the way I doubted Gunner could?

It didn't matter. I'd face death head-on before I admitted who Petrov was to anyone.

He released my neck, drew back with his right hand and struck, putting a hole in the bedroom wall. I didn't shrink away from him.

Gunner took a step back. "Come with me." He left the room and stalked down the hall without bothering to see whether I was following. On his way, he grabbed a shirt that he'd tossed over the back of a chair and pulled it over his head.

When he reached the house's main room, he pointed to one of the sofas. *"Sit,"* he told me.

I ignored him and stood with my arms folded.

"When were you born?"

"You already know the answer."

"What day? You don't know, do you?"

I didn't answer or even move my head.

"Who were you before the KGB recruited you?"

I couldn't find my voice to answer him.

"Who is Zaryana Ivashov?"

This time I squared my shoulders, but still didn't speak.

"Who is Petrov to you?" he repeated.

Inside, I was trembling with a combination of fear and uncertainty. When Gunner walked closer, I wasn't sure what he intended to do. Part of me still believed he wouldn't strike me, but without another wall in close enough proximity, maybe I should consider the possibility that he would.

I didn't flinch when he raised his arm and stroked the side of my face with his finger. My eyes met his, and I wished I knew what he was thinking.

"Rocket Girl," he murmured. "Why can't you just tell me the truth? Why can't you believe I want to help you?"

Of everything he'd said, yelled, or demanded of me, that statement affected me the most. I bit down on my tongue as my stupid eyes filled with tears. When I tried to move away, Gunner wrapped his arms around me and pulled me close. "I need you to know something."

I nodded.

"I want you, Rocket Girl, and I think you want me just as bad."

I lowered my gaze.

"Look at me, dammit."

I stared into his eyes, wondering if he knew what having his arms around me was doing to me. Did he know that I was aroused? Could he tell?

"I need you to know that whatever might happen between us physically, has nothing to do with the questions I'm asking you. Do you understand what I mean?"

I nodded a second time.

"I want to kiss you so fucking bad."

"Then, do it."

"If I do, the next step will be stripping you naked and taking you to bed, but first I have to know that you understand this is separate. That you trust me."

His eyes bored into mine. I longed for him to just do everything he'd said. Not ask, not make me answer.

17

Gunner

I could physically feel her hesitancy and wished I had the words to convince her to trust me. Even if she didn't answer a single one of my questions, I still needed to hear her voice.

Instead of waiting any longer, I covered her mouth with mine, pushing my tongue inside and making it impossible for her to speak.

What she said with her lips and her tongue, though, told me what I needed to know for now. When she pressed her body against mine, I released the grip I had on her, picked her up, and carried her to my bedroom.

"Tell me you want this," I said before crossing over the threshold.

Raketa nodded.

"Not good enough, Rocket Girl. I need to hear the words. Tell me you want this. Tell me you understand that what is about to happen doesn't have a damn thing to do with Petrov, United Russia, K19, or anything else that is happening outside the walls of this room."

"I understand."

I still didn't move. That wasn't enough. I needed to hear the rest.

"I want this," she whispered.

I walked over to the bed and rested her body on it. "Lean back for me." I hovered over her, making sure she watched everything I was doing.

With one arm resting on my elbow, I unfastened the buttons on her shirt with the other. It was one of many I'd picked out for her when my sister, who owned a women's clothing store, sent me an email with options for the woman I'd described to her.

"She's probably a size zero, the way you've described her. I'll send a mix of that and one size up."

I'd thanked her and agreed to tell her more as soon as I could. She was used to that line both from me and our father, who had retired as a four-star general.

"Look at you," I murmured when I unfastened the last button and opened her shirt, exposing the soft skin of her belly and the pale pink of the bra my sister had also sent.

Raketa's eyes remained on mine as I leaned forward and licked my way from her belly button up to the thin clasp that held together the cups of her bra. She took in a breath when I released it and let it fall to the side. I ran my tongue around her dusty-rose nipples, gently nibbling each one before continuing my trail of kisses up her sternum, to her neck, and finally to her mouth.

I'd been gentle to that point, but I couldn't hold back any longer. I kissed her hard, battling her tongue with mine, increasing the pressure as she responded the same way.

I reached around and pulled the shirt I'd just put on over my head and dropped my shorts.

"I'm sweaty," I said, but the heat in her eyes told me it didn't matter.

I stood, resting one knee on the bed, next to her, and pulled down her elastic-waist workout shorts, smiling when I saw she was wearing the matching pale-pink panties.

It didn't matter that Raketa was one of the most badass Russian operatives who'd ever lived; underneath it all, she was a woman who could be soft and sweet and sexy as all get-out.

I lay on the bed next to her and licked the skin above the waistband of her panties before grasping each side and pulling them down her legs and off her body.

The scent of her arousal was so powerful I couldn't resist a taste. "Let me do this," I said when she squirmed.

Raketa opened her legs wider.

"More," I demanded. "That's better," I said when she did.

I brought my mouth to her flesh, and every muscle in her body tensed.

"Talk to me, Rocket Girl," I murmured.

Raketa closed her eyes, her face flushed, and she turned her head away.

I moved up her body and grasped her chin. "Don't. Talk to me."

She shook her head and didn't open her eyes.

I kissed her again, pushing my tongue into her mouth.

"That's you, how you taste," I said. "And I want more."

The muscles that had relaxed tightened again. I stroked her cheek with my finger and brought my lips to hers a second time. I kissed her softly and then continued down her neck until I reached her breasts. Equally gentle, I laved one nipple while my fingers teased the other. Little by little, her tension released.

As soon as I moved down her body farther, she tensed again.

"I wish you would talk to me," I said, looking up at her. "Did someone…"

When her eyes filled with tears, I stopped talking, stopped my mouth's assault on her body, and held her close, resting my head on her stomach.

"I've never…" Her words were barely a whisper.

"Do you trust me, Rocket Girl?"

What I saw in her eyes wasn't just about sex. She didn't trust me at all, and she couldn't lie to me and say that she did. I respected that.

Again, I stroked her face with my finger and gently kissed her. I didn't do more than that and didn't intend to.

"I'm sorry," she said when, after several minutes, I stood, picked her clothes up off the floor, and handed them to her. "We can still—"

"No, sweetheart. We can't. Not until you trust me." I pulled on my shorts and sat on the edge of the bed with my back to her. "I'm the one who's sorry. I shouldn't have…"

What could I say? I'd asked her to tell me she understood that sex between us was separate from me wanting to know what she was involved in or up against. I had to make sure that she understood I wasn't using intimacy to get her to talk. I should've also asked about her trust before I brought her in here, stripped her of her clothes, and made her vulnerable to me.

I felt her weight leave the bed and heard the door close behind her. I put my t-shirt back on but didn't immediately follow her out of the bedroom. I'd give Raketa a few minutes, or maybe the rest of the day. I'd handled this all wrong. How could she believe anything other than that I was trying to manipulate her?

It wasn't just that I was being noble with Raketa; I believed the words I'd said to her. Sure, there had been women I wasn't in a relationship with that I'd had sex with. There'd been no question in my mind that they knew the score and didn't expect anything more from me.

With Raketa, though, it was different. Just like it would've been different with Lena, not that we'd ever been intimate. We'd come close, back before her accident. In hindsight, we'd never had a chance. She hadn't just been in denial about her relationship with her ex-husband; she had been obsessed with him. Why had I been so blind to it?

Was I being equally blind when it came to Raketa? I wanted her, and it wasn't just because I hadn't had sex with anyone since the night she and I were together.

God, I hated that I couldn't remember more from that night. I'd been drunk off my ass. If I had it to go back and do over again, I wouldn't lay a hand on her.

I looked up when Raketa walked back into the room.

"There's something more I need to say," I said before she had a chance to speak.

She walked closer. "Go ahead."

"That night, you know, when we were together. We shouldn't have had sex. I was drunk. That is a piss-poor excuse, but it's the truth. I wish I could go back and undo it, but I can't. I'm sorry for that."

Raketa opened her mouth and closed it again before turning away from me and stalking out of the bedroom a second time.

"Wait," I said, running after her and grabbing her arm. "I'm trying to be a gentleman here. I know you don't trust me, and if what we did that night is part of it, I want you to know that I'm sorry."

She scrunched her eyes, her lips drew tightly together, and she wrenched her arm from my grasp.

"Fuck you," she spat before running into the woods.

18

Zary

If he followed me, he would live to regret it. Maybe. As mad as I was, I just might kill him. *We shouldn't have had sex?* How awesome that I'd lost my virginity at the age of thirty to a man who wished it never happened. If I'd known then what I knew now, I could've had sex with *anyone.* It would've mattered just as much as it had with Gunner—which wasn't at all.

"Hey, wait a minute," I heard him say. He was right behind me, but I kept walking. *"Zaryana."*

I spun around on him. "Don't call me that. Not ever again. *Do you understand?*" I used the same condescending voice he had with me.

"Wait," he repeated, grabbing my arm more firmly than before, perhaps knowing I'd try to get away from him. He pulled me against him and held me tightly enough that he could turn me around and encircle me in his arms.

"Let me go. I don't want this," I said, refusing to look at his stupid, smug, beautiful face or the stupid green eyes that made me melt.

"First, I won't ever call you that again, although I wish I understood why you don't want me to; it's a beautiful name. Second, as I *said,* I was trying to be a gentleman. I was apologizing."

"Etmez."

The look on Gunner's face made me realize my mistake. I'd spoken in Azeri, not Russian.

"Release me."

Gunner shook his head. "Were you his lover?"

I pushed at him with all my might, and he let go. *"Fuck you,"* I spat again, running farther into the woods.

Jesus. Is that what he thought, that I'd had sex with that disgusting piece of shit not worthy to be called a human being? The idea of it made me want to puke.

When I got to the water's edge, I bent over and put my hands on my knees. My stomach was empty of food, but I expelled the bile that rose in my throat. Too soon I felt Gunner's hand on my back.

"Can't you leave me alone? *Please, just leave me alone,*" I cried.

"No. I can't, and not for the reason you think."

"There needs to be no reason for you not to leave a woman alone who asks it of you." I hated the sound of my voice. I was angry and when I was, my accent grew stronger and it became harder for me to get the words right in English.

Instead of walking away, Gunner swept me into his arms.

"*What are you fucking doing*? Put me down," I shouted, punching at his chest.

"We're going to talk, and you can stop with the bad language; it has no effect on me. I don't talk to you that way."

"*You are not my superior. You don't tell me how to speak. You are not my fath—*"

I knew the instant Gunner realized who Makar Petrov was to me. He set me on my feet but kept his arm tightly around me.

"He's your father."

I tried to hide the pain, the utter despair I felt, having to admit he was right. And I hated him for being able to see right through me.

"Tell me about him."

I closed my eyes and forced away the emotion I was feeling. I recognized that too. I'd been trained not to show a reaction of any kind. I knew how to rein myself in.

"You're wrong. He was not my lover nor is he my father," I lied.

"What I should've said earlier, but didn't, was that I wish, so much, that the first time I felt your skin against mine, I had been completely sober. I wish that when I close my eyes, I could remember every inch of your body, exactly how you felt. I remember, but not enough. And I hate that."

"You don't remember anything." Why was he bringing this up again now, when he'd just all but gotten me to admit I was Petrov's daughter?

"I'm sorry, Rocket Girl. The last thing I want to do is hurt you."

"Let me go."

He dropped his hands to his sides.

"From here. Let me leave."

He shook his head. "You're here for your own protection. Until we can—"

"The same words Petrov used. How does it make you feel to know you think the same way as that monster?"

He stood perfectly still, but didn't look at all insulted by my words. I could tell what was on his mind, though.

"You think that you're keeping me safe from UR, aren't you? Well, so was he. You're thinking he didn't give me a choice when he took me to Azerbaijan. Neither did you when you brought me here. You are no different. Don't kid yourself into thinking you are."

I left him standing on the beach and went back to the house, where I could at least close the door of the bedroom and be alone.

My words did nothing to thwart him. I knew Gunner would not let me leave, and without a way to communicate with anyone other than him, I was trapped on this island. I couldn't swim my way to freedom. Even if I could, once I arrived, I had no one to help me anyway.

United Russia wanted me dead. Petrov wanted me to deliver his *daughters*, and whether I did or not, I'd end up dead anyway. There wasn't a doubt in my mind that if I somehow managed the impossible and abducted the two women, as soon as I handed them over, Petrov would kill me.

I couldn't go to the CIA for help, because they worked with Gunner.

I'd always been alone in the world, but not like I was now. The only way I could stay alive would be to remain on this island with a man I was quickly coming to despise.

Gunner stayed away from me the rest of the day. I heard him come and go, but I didn't leave the bedroom unless I was certain he was outside, and then, it was only to use the restroom or get some water.

It would be dark soon, and he would likely be inside for the rest of the night. Eventually, I'd be forced to talk to him, and I still hadn't figured out what I'd say.

I could ask again to be let go, but that would be a waste of breath. He'd never let me; he was *protecting* me.

I jumped when I heard a knock on the door and waited for it to open. It didn't, and while I hadn't heard his approach, I did hear him walking away.

After a while, my stomach started to rumble. I kicked myself for not getting food earlier when I was sure he was still outside.

The pangs in my stomach grew worse when the smell of whatever Gunner was cooking wafted into the room. It smelled divine, and I couldn't remember the last time I ate. I lasted five more minutes before I opened the bedroom door and walked into the kitchen.

Gunner didn't say anything, but he did stand, walk over to the oven, take out a covered plate, and set it in front of me.

Beneath the cover he removed was grilled salmon, rice, and vegetables.

"It's really good," I said after several mouthfuls. "Thank you."

When he didn't respond, I looked up at him.

"You're welcome. Would you like more?"

"Yes, please," I muttered. "I can get it, though."

"Yeah? Know your way around a kitchen?"

He was teasing me, and I appreciated his effort to lighten the tension between us. "Actually, I don't."

"Good," he said, standing and taking my plate. "It'll give us something to do."

"What do you mean?"

"I'll teach you how to cook."

"Oh, uh…"

He set the plate down in front of me and then went back to his seat across the table. "Look at me," he said, waiting for me to do as he asked before continuing. "Got a better idea?"

When my eyes met his, my mind filled with several better ideas. How could my body respond so quickly when a few short hours ago I couldn't imagine ever wanting to look at him again? I looked down at my plate and raised another forkful to my mouth.

"Yeah, I can think of a lot of better ideas too," he muttered, almost causing me to drop my fork. "Listen, I think we should start over. Things got out of hand earlier."

I nodded. "I agree."

"That things got out of hand or that we should start over?"

"Both."

"Good." Gunner finished the food on his plate and took it to the sink. "When you're done eating, I'll build a fire and we can sit outside."

"Thank you, Gunner."

"You're welcome." He left the kitchen and went out the front door.

I could tell by the heaviness of his footfalls that he was still angry, but at least he'd given me an opening for us to talk again.

19

Gunner

It was probably shitty of me to leave the way I had, but if I hadn't, I would've been all over her.

Raketa was the first person I'd shared a meal with at my kitchen table. When Razor and Shiv had been here, each time, we sat outside or in the living room when we ate. It felt good, looking up and seeing her across from me. That feeling had quickly changed, though. As my eyes took in her thin frame and I watched her take mouthfuls of food I'd made for her, something I could only describe as primal came over me.

If I'd stayed in that room with her another minute, I would've thrown her over my shoulder, carried her into the bedroom, and torn the clothes from her body. Only after I'd looked my fill of her naked flesh, would I sink my body into hers in the way I longed to.

Going caveman on her would most likely result in me never earning her trust, which was why I'd left the way I did.

Her reaction earlier, before everything between us went to hell, puzzled me.

It was as though she'd never experienced oral sex before. I kicked the pile of logs in front of me when I couldn't remember whether I'd gone down on her or not the night we were together.

Probably not, since she left the next morning without so much as a "see ya later." Also, given how inebriated I was, maybe the sex had sucked, and not in a good way.

I adjusted my shorts, knowing that if I didn't quit thinking about a do-over, she'd probably slap my face before she stormed back inside and sequestered herself in the bedroom for the remainder of the night.

I stacked the logs in the pit, lit a fire, and then pulled two Adirondack chairs to the other side of it so the shifting breeze wouldn't blow smoke our way.

Just when I'd decided she wasn't going to join me, I heard the front door open.

"Hey, there," I said, looking her up and down. "Cold?" When I left, she'd been wearing the same pair of shorts and shirt I'd stripped from her body earlier. Now she had on a pair of jeans and a long-sleeve shirt.

It was probably better that she'd changed, given my body's reaction to remembering stripping her.

I motioned to the chair next to me, and she sat down.

I struggled with what to say; I was terrible at small talk. Sure, I knew how to flirt, but given the circumstances, that probably wouldn't be the best approach. What, though, did we have to talk about? I couldn't ask her about her childhood, or even much about her life.

"Do you remember the first time we saw each other?" she asked, startling me.

"I do." I closed my eyes, remembering that moment and how it had shaken me. "You took my breath away."

"I didn't think you'd remember," she mumbled.

"You didn't kill me. That's hard to forget."

"Oh, right. I did have a gun pointed at you; that would take anyone's breath away."

I leaned forward. "That isn't what I meant, Rocket Girl." I stroked my finger down the side of her face. "It was the feeling I got when I looked into your eyes."

"I couldn't pull the trigger. That had never happened to me before."

"Why do you think that was?"

"I don't know. I've asked myself many times."

"It was like we'd met before. Another time, maybe."

Raketa laughed. "Like in another life?"

I shrugged. "I can't say I believe in shit like that, but yeah. I can't explain the way I felt. It happens every time I see you."

"It's the same for me," she said, almost too quietly for me to hear.

I leaned in closer, unable to resist brushing her lips with mine. She put one hand on the back of my neck and rested the other near my heart.

She pulled back. "I want to trust you. I don't know how. I've never done it before."

I studied her beautiful features. "That is the most honest thing you've ever said to me." I kissed her again, this time deeper, with more of the passion I was trying so hard to rein in.

I sat back and looked up at the stars. "I don't want to do the wrong thing. Other than when I've been working an op and doing the wrong thing would mean either I or someone on my team would die, I don't remember feeling this way. At least not as strongly. I feel like I'm walking on eggshells."

"I don't understand."

"I'm afraid of saying the wrong thing."

"I'm sorry."

"Don't be. I just want you to know that this is important to me. You're important to me." I shook my head. "I'm not accustomed to saying that."

"I don't think I've ever said it," she admitted.

"Raketa, I…"

She waited while I struggled with what I wanted to say.

"Earlier…what I said…I don't know how to apologize without making it worse. Not for us being together, but for making you think I regretted it."

"Don't you?"

I leaned forward again. "Not in the way you're thinking right now. I regret that I didn't take better care of you…" I laughed. "I'm sorry I wasn't a better lover."

Raketa smiled, but just slightly. "So certain it was terrible. That's how I know you don't remember."

"I don't know what your benchmark is, but I can assure you, I can do better."

"My what? A mark?"

"It means something to measure against, like a comparison."

"Ah. I don't have a benchmark, Gunner. I didn't before that night, and I still don't."

I scrubbed my face with my hand. Did she mean what I thought she did? Nah, that couldn't be.

"Now I'm the one who doesn't understand."

"You're the only man I've been with."

Jesus—and I was drunk. I felt like the biggest asshole who'd ever lived, and I had no idea what to say. I rested my head against the back of the chair and looked up at the stars a second time. I couldn't say I was sorry again. What would she think I was sorry for? "I'm back to not having any idea what to say."

"There isn't anything—"

When she stood and it appeared she was heading inside, I grabbed her and pulled her into my lap. I gripped one side of her face while I held her tight to me with my other hand. I struggled with words and then gave up. Instead, I'd use my mouth in another way to tell her how I felt.

I kissed her, harder than I had before. I explored her mouth with my tongue, wanting to know every crevice, every hidden inch of her body. Tonight I would, because tonight I would do what I should've done the first time we were together.

I stood with her still in my arms and carried her into the house.

"I want you to trust me. Just this, Raketa. Trust this," I said as I laid her body on the bed.

She nodded, the look in her eyes equally heated and anxious.

I hovered above her. "Tonight won't just be sex, Rocket Girl. I'm going to learn as much as I can about your body, and you're going to do the same with mine."

"Okay," she whispered.

"Let me," I said when I saw her reaching for the waistband of her jeans. "And when I'm finished, you'll take mine off."

She rested against the pillows, her eyes focused on my hands and the way I undressed her. When her clothes were off and she lay naked in front of me, I ran my hands from her neck, slowly, down her body. I kept my touch gentle, soaking in the feel of her through the tips of my fingers.

"Your turn," I said when I reached her toes.

I stood and helped her off the bed.

She grabbed the bottom of my shirt and pushed it up and over my head. She pushed my shorts down my body and knelt in front of me as I stepped out of them.

"Come with me," I said, pulling her toward the bathroom. I flipped a switch and the room was awash with a soft glow, almost like candlelight.

I left her standing by the bath after I started the water, and walked over to the fireplace and lit it.

"I hope you took a long nap today, because I don't think I'll be able to let you sleep tonight."

She smiled and I helped her climb into the warm water and then joined her.

"I need you closer," I said, pulling her to sit between my legs.

I drizzled body wash on the front of her and took my time massaging it into her full breasts. Her body began to shake.

"Gunner," she whispered. "I want…I ache."

My fingers trailed closer to the heat between her legs, and she whimpered.

"What was that, Rocket Girl?"

"I want," she moaned a second time. "But I don't know what I want. Just don't stop."

"I don't plan to."

When I stroked her clit with my finger, Raketa jolted. The more I toyed with her, the harder I knew it was for her not to squirm away from my touch.

"Let me do this," I said, thrusting two fingers inside of her while the pad of my thumb rested against the most sensitive part of her body.

"Come for me, Rocket Girl," I whispered, curling my fingers inside of her.

"Gunner, oh my God," she moaned, digging her fingers into my thighs as she rode the wave of pleasure streaming through her body.

She rested against me and I ran my fingers over her hardened nipples. I started slowly but was soon relentless in my exploration of her body, running my hands over every inch, from her neck to her legs.

I wound my hand in her hair and released the tight bun she usually kept it in.

"I love your hair," I murmured as I watched the long locks touch the water. "I've only seen you with it down once, and ever since, I've fantasized about seeing you this way, but naked, and just for me."

She whimpered again.

"What was that?" I murmured, kissing her neck just below her ear.

"It feels so good."

"What does? This?" I ran my tongue down her neck to her shoulder. "Or this?" My fingers dug into her scalp.

"Everything. I never…"

"Tell me. Don't keep anything inside. Tell me everything you're thinking. Tell me how I make you feel, Raketa."

"I didn't know it would be like this."

"I'm glad."

"Why?"

"Because I'm the only one who's made you feel this way."

The feeling of possessiveness that washed over me took me by surprise. I was back to being a caveman, wanting to claim her as my own and never let anyone else ever touch her the way I was.

Her body responded to me like it was made to feel my fingers. With every whimper, every moan, every squirm I felt myself harden to the point where I ached the same way she said she did.

"I want to be inside you," I whispered.

She moved away from me, but I pulled her back.

I reached over the side of the tub and pressed the control for the shower. I hadn't used this particular option before, but it was perfect. Instead of water raining down, the flow encircled us.

"Stay right where you are," I said, moving her to the tub's edge. "I'll be right back."

"Where are you going?"

"To get a condom, sweetheart. Don't move." I rested my gaze on her nakedness. As much as I wanted to feel her wrapped around me with nothing between us, I couldn't risk getting her pregnant when she was trusting me to take care of her.

As I padded my way to the bedroom, a terrible thought crossed my mind. Had I used a condom when we were together before? I couldn't remember.

Later, we'd talk about it. Now wasn't the time to bring up the night she'd given me the gift of herself and I was too drunk to appreciate it.

I grabbed the unopened box from the drawer of my nightstand and silently thanked Razor for giving me a gift we both thought was a joke as a housewarming present.

When I walked back into the bathroom and saw her sitting right where I'd left her with the glow of the fire illuminating her through the stream of water, I stopped moving and soaked in every inch of her nakedness.

Instead of taking her there like I'd planned, I walked over, turned off the water, and gathered her in my arms. The caveman was back. I wanted her in my bed tonight and every night from then on.

I felt the chill on her skin and held her closer. "Let's get you warm."

"I feel like I'm already on fire."

"Hang on, baby, soon it'll feel like an inferno."

I sat down on the bed with her still in my arms, opened the box, and pulled out a foil packet.

"Next time, I'll let you do this, but right now, I feel like I'll explode if you even touch me," I said when she reached for it.

I shifted her off my lap, sheathed myself, and then rested my body between her legs.

"Eyes open," I said when she closed them. "Keep them on mine. I want you to see what you do to me when I'm inside you."

She nodded and bit her bottom lip.

"There's nothing to be afraid of. I promised to take care of you, and I will."

It was all I could do to keep my eyes open the way I'd told her to when I eased inside of her body. Now

I understood why I'd remembered her tightness when there were so many other details I couldn't recall.

I moved slowly, gently, waiting as her body adjusted to my size. I prayed I hadn't hurt her the first time we were together, but refused to let the thought eclipse what was happening between us now.

Raketa wrapped her legs around me and dug her fingers into my thighs.

"I want more," she groaned, thrusting her body against mine, pushing me over the edge to a place where I couldn't be gentle, couldn't take it slow like I wanted to. I met her gaze as I pounded into her, waiting until the moment I knew she was about to take off before I let myself go with her.

20

Zary

I opened my eyes. The sun was just beginning to rise; I could see its glow through the windows Gunner had no reason to cover.

His head rested on my chest, and I ran my fingers through his hair, massaging his scalp gently, not wanting to wake him.

As he'd warned, we didn't sleep until maybe a half hour ago when we finally fell into each other's arms and closed our eyes.

Gunner gave me more pleasure than I'd ever dreamed possible, and taught me how to give to him as well. He'd explored my body with his eyes, his hands, and his mouth, and then let me do the same to his.

I thought back to when I'd asked if he remembered the first time we saw each other. I was shocked that he did, but more when he said it had moved him in the same way it had me.

He joked about us knowing each other in a past life, something I didn't believe in either, but what other explanation could there be for the way I felt when I was with him?

I giggled when I felt his tongue on my tummy. "You're awake."

"Your body is naked under mine. How could I sleep?" He raised his head and scooted closer. "Kiss me," he demanded, so I did.

Gunner rolled to his back and brought me with him. He reached over to the box of condoms, pulled one out, and handed it to me.

"Have your way with me, Rocket Girl." He dropped his hands to his sides in surrender and winked.

I had no words to describe the way I felt this morning. My life had been filled with far more misery than happiness, but I recognized the warmth in my chest. How many times had I laughed, smiled, even giggled in the last few hours? More than I had in the rest of my life combined.

I rolled the condom over his length and straddled him. He held my waist, easing me onto him more slowly than I would've.

"Are you sore?" he asked when he was seated deep inside me.

"A little," I answered, starting to move.

"Take it slow," he said, forcing me to with his guiding hands.

"What happened to letting me have my way with you?"

Gunner moved his hands from my waist and covered my breasts with them.

"I don't want to hurt you."

"Then, be still."

I closed my eyes, waiting for him to tell me to watch him, but he didn't. Instead, I let myself get lost in how my pussy stretched and pulled him inside of me.

When he wrapped his hands in my long hair and pulled, my body tightened and then exploded. I leaned forward and rested my head on his chest.

"I'm hungry," I murmured a few minutes later.

He put his hands around my waist. "You're starving, actually." He rolled me off him, stood, and held his hand out. "Time for your first cooking lesson. What do you like for breakfast?"

I sat up. "Not much, usually just some fruit."

"Well, you can't cook that. Wait, I guess you could, but why would you? Today we'll have bacon and eggs, or would you prefer pancakes?"

"I'd prefer fruit," I grumbled. "It's quicker."

An hour later, we sat down to the worst breakfast I'd ever eaten. The eggs were watery and the bacon was black, but Gunner said it was perfect. I'd tried, and that was all he wanted, he told me.

"I was thinking I could show you around the island if you're up for it," he said after I insisted on cleaning the kitchen while he relaxed and watched.

"I'd like that."

"We're almost there," he turned back and said. "You doin' okay?"

We were walking through a beautiful forest. I wasn't hunting someone United Russia wanted me to kill. There hadn't been a time in my life that I could remember being more okay than I was now. Every so often, I found myself humming a tune I remembered my mother singing to me. When was the last time I'd hummed, if ever?

"Here it is," said Gunner, reaching for my hand and then putting his arm around my shoulders when I stood next to him.

Before me was a beautiful waterfall. At its bottom was a pool of water with lush vegetation growing on its banks. I couldn't explain why, but my eyes filled with tears.

"I reacted that way the first time I saw it," Gunner said, catching a teardrop on his fingertip. "Up for a swim?"

Before I could protest, Gunner had his shirt off and was pulling down his shorts.

"Come swim with me, Rocket Girl," he said, holding his hand out to me.

How could I resist a man whose body brought me to my knees and made me weep more than the waterfall. I'd never seen anyone with a more perfect physique than Gunner, and that was with clothes on. Naked he looked like a god.

I shed my clothes and climbed into the pool, surprised at how warm the water was. I took the tie out of my hair, closed my eyes, and sat beneath the flow of the waterfall. It felt like Gunner's shower, but so much better.

When I opened my eyes, Gunner was standing close enough to touch me, but he hadn't.

"If I live to be one hundred and I forget every other thing about my life, I will never forget this moment."

My cheeks flushed and I looked down into the water. Gunner cupped my face and brought his lips to mine.

"Thank you," I said when he pulled away.

"For?"

"I shouldn't have to explain." I smiled. "But I will." I took a deep breath. "Thank you for bringing me here. Thank you for caring about me." My eyes filled with tears again, and I tried to look away.

"Hey," he said, grasping my chin. "Why are you crying?"

"You'll think I'm feeling sorry for myself," I whispered.

"Tell me anyway."

"Before…when I asked you to let me leave, I realized something."

Gunner's eyes bored into mine so intensely I hesitated before continuing.

"Tell me."

"I don't have anyone," I admitted as tears ran down my cheeks. "If you let me go, I wouldn't know what to do."

"You have me."

"Gunner…I…"

"You do, Raketa. You've known that for a long time. Deep inside your heart, you knew you could trust me. That's why you asked me to help you get away from United Russia. You knew I would."

Every word he said was true. I had known.

"I'm lucky," he began. "I always have been. I may not be the easiest guy to get along with, but Razor, Doc, and Mercer have always had my back, no matter how much of an asshole I am to them. I know it's different for you, Rocket Girl."

He looked into my eyes. "You're not alone any-more. It isn't just me; the K19 team is behind you too. They put you first when we raided the compound. The first part of the mission was rescuing you. Getting to Petrov was second."

"Honestly?"

Gunner nodded.

"But why?"

He shrugged. "I guess they knew how I felt about you even without me telling them."

Did I dare ask what that meant? Could I bear hearing the words I'd never dreamed I would, and not dissolve into a puddle of emotion?

Gunner brought his forehead to mine. "I can't explain it. I told you that last night, but it's true. You have a pull on me that I couldn't ignore even if I wanted to, and I don't want to. I want you here with me, and that has nothing to do with any mission I've ever accepted."

I put my arms around him and held my body close to his. "Thank you, Gunner," I whispered for the second time.

"I know there's something you can't tell me yet, but I believe one day you'll be able to. In the meantime, I'm not going to push. You're safe here, and while you say that Petrov said the same thing to you—"

"I'm sorry I said that."

"Wait and hear me out. I know why you said it, and after you did, I thought long and hard about whether what I was doing was the same as what he did. I decided that it isn't."

"I know it isn't."

"Here's why. All I care about is keeping you safe. That's it. I know there will come a time when we have to leave this island, but for now, I don't want to think about when that might be."

"Me either."

"So, how about we pretend the rest of the world doesn't exist for a while?"

I didn't need to ask if he really meant it; I knew he did.

"Let's go back now," he said.

"Why?"

"Because I want you so bad it hurts," he said, rubbing himself against me.

"I want you too." I shifted so I could wrap my legs around his waist.

"We can't."

"Why not?"

"I didn't pack the condoms."

I reached over to where I'd left my shorts. "I did."

21

Gunner

Sex under the waterfall on my island had to have been the single-most exhilarating, erotic thing I'd ever done. As I led Raketa through the trees, the thought occurred to me that I hadn't brought any condoms with me. That she had was practically like…winning a million bucks.

She was quiet on the walk back to the house, but I didn't feel as though things were awkward between us. The silence felt natural.

"Hungry?" I asked when we walked inside.

Raketa had been looking out the window, but turned to look at me and shrugged. "Are you?"

"You don't eat enough."

She chuckled, sort of. "That would've been the appropriate answer if I'd asked why you asked if I'm hungry."

I smiled. "No, Rocket Girl, I'm not hungry."

She smiled too. "Why did you say I don't eat enough?"

I moved closer and put my hands on her waist. "Because I can feel your bones."

A pained look flashed on her face.

"What did I say?"

"Food wasn't always…plentiful."

I nodded. "If I asked you to tell me about your life would you think it's because I'm interested or because I'm trying to get information?"

Raketa sat down at the kitchen table. "It isn't a very interesting story."

I pulled another chair closer to her. "Everything about you is interesting to me."

"I doubt there's anything I could tell you that you don't already know."

She was right, at least after she'd turned eighteen. Prior to that, there was nothing. If I asked about that, though, it would be solely to get information.

"I may know the facts, but I know nothing about what you were like, how you felt, what *your* life was actually like."

"I told you—boring."

I nodded again. "I'll tell you about my life, then."

Raketa folded her arms when I leaned back in my chair. What was she afraid I would tell her? Something made her take a step back, close herself off to me.

"I have one sibling, a sister. She picked out your clothes, by the way."

She raised an eyebrow.

"She owns a clothing store," I explained.

"Thank you."

I nodded once more. "Her name is Odette."

"Interesting name."

"Both my parents are French, although my dad was born in the States."

"Is Gunner a French name?"

I laughed. "No, my father was a military man. I'm surprised you don't know that."

"Oliver Marchand Godet. Retired four-star general. Deceased at the age of sixty-two," she murmured.

She rattled off the basic statistics of my father's life with no emotion, just like she would've in a briefing. My dad was so much more than her words.

"He was the best man I ever knew."

"Tell me about him," she said, uncrossing her arms and resting them on the table.

I told her about the first time my father brought me to the island along with several other stories about growing up with the man who was known as "Devil Dog."

"He wasn't around a lot, but he always made up for it when he was on leave."

"And your mother?"

"Salt of the earth, as you'd expect any son to say, but in this case, it's true. Nothing fazes the woman, or if it does, I've never seen her show it."

"You're like her."

I laughed again. "I would've expected you to say I'm her polar opposite."

Raketa tilted her head.

"Most would say everything fazes me."

"I don't agree. You're very, what is the expression? Even-keeled?"

"If you think so, you don't know me very well."

I saw the flash of hurt in her eyes that she quickly masked.

"I was joking," I said, taking her hand in mine. "You've seen sides of me very few have."

"No one…" She shook her head.

I leaned forward and kissed her. "I'll finish your sentence for you. There's no one I wanted to share my house with more than you."

She scrunched her eyes.

"It's true, Rocket Girl. I like having you here."

"I like being here," she whispered.

"You don't have to be tentative with me. You'd know if I was lying to you. You'd also know if I didn't want you here."

"I'm not sure about knowing you were lying to me."

"Sure, you would. Just like I know when you're lying to me."

I waited. I was taking a risk, hoping that if I opened up to her, she might do the same. At least a little.

She took a deep breath, studying me.

"Trust me," I whispered.

"I want to."

"I won't ask, Raketa. Whatever you want to tell me will be in your own time. I just hope, one day soon, you'll trust me enough to tell me where your pain comes from."

She stood, walked across the kitchen, and looked out the window. "It's really beautiful here."

"I agree." The leaves were just beginning to change. Soon the entire island would be awash with the reds, oranges, and yellows of autumn, and shortly after that, the days would become increasingly colder.

"I grew up in a children's home," she began without turning around to look at me.

I waited, steadfast in my commitment not to ask her questions.

"When I was young, my parents were killed."

"That's what you were told."

She nodded, still not turning around to look at me.

"I was taken to Moscow."

"From Azerbaijan."

She nodded again, this time facing me. "I became a child of the SVR."

"When you were eighteen."

"Before that. I was seventeen."

I nodded.

"That's when I became Raketa. I left Zaryana behind."

"Raketa Ivashov."

"My mother's maiden name."

"I see."

"This is what you wanted to know, yes?"

I stood and walked over to her. "No," I said, pulling her close to me.

"Petrov has my mother."

I took a deep breath and kissed her forehead. "You want to go back and get her."

Raketa rested her head against my chest and nodded.

"Then, that's what we'll do."

She pulled away from me. "Are you serious? As easy as that?"

"I'll arrange a meeting."

"With?"

"Let's start with K19. We'll determine what help we'll need from there."

"Why?"

"You're asking why I'm willing to help you extract your mother?"

Raketa nodded, waiting for me to answer, but I didn't right away. Instead, I kissed her.

I wove my hand into her hair as our kiss intensified. I put my hands on her bottom, and she wrapped her legs around my waist. I carried her into the bedroom.

"Gunner?"

"Shh," I said, lowering her body to the bed.

If she asked, I wouldn't be able to explain why. The only way I knew how to tell her why I was willing to help her risk her life and mine by going back into Petrov's compound, was by joining our bodies together. Maybe because I hoped she realized that what we had was so much more than sex.

From undressing her to bringing her to the brink of ultimate pleasure again and again, I took my time.

This wasn't sex. I was making love to the woman in my arms. Did she know that this was different without me having to say so? If I spoke now, my words might terrify her because when she wanted to know why, the only answer that came to mind was that I loved her.

Did she know when I kissed each of her eyelids, or the tip of her nose, or her forehead, that to me, they were the most precious kisses I'd ever given anyone?

As I ran my hands over the stiff peaks of her nipples, or down her sides, or along the soft skin of her tummy, did she know I'd never trail my fingertips over anyone's naked flesh again, other than hers?

When I felt her shudder as I brought my mouth to her pussy, did she know that her taste was the only one I'd know for the rest of my life?

When my cock rested inside her, did she know that I'd never penetrate another woman's body with mine ever again?

When words of affection escaped her lips without her realizing it, did she know that I understood Azeri and that I knew she was feeling everything I was?

"Look at me," I said when her eyes drifted closed. When they opened, their vividness burned a hole through my skin and into my heart.

"I'd die for you, Rocket Girl."

"And I, you."

"I…"

She rested her fingertips on my lips. "Shh," she said, repeating what I'd told her earlier.

In that moment, I knew what I had to do. I'd told her we'd meet with the K19 team together, but we wouldn't.

"Hey, Raze," I said when my buddy answered my call. "Petrov is Ivashov's father. The woman being held on his compound is her mother."

"Shiv has been on standby, waiting for your confirmation."

"Tell him I'm ready."

"Good work, man."

"Let me know when Mantis will be here."

"Roger that."

22

Zary

When Gunner crept from the bed, I continued to pretend I was asleep. Talking to him now was out of the question. If I did, I'd tell him every secret I'd ever held close, every detail about the first thirty years of my life, and every single dream I'd had of him. Instead, I let him close the door on my unspoken words.

I slid from under the sheets of his bed and tiptoed into the bathroom. From there, I could see him outside, on his phone, anxiously running the fingers of one hand through his hair.

Was he calling his K19 teammates to arrange for their help as he'd told me, or was he betraying the confidences I'd shared with him?

Doubt ate at me, and I hated it.

When I finally came out of the room, Gunner was nowhere to be found. I'd watched him walk through the woods after he stuck his phone in the waistband of his shorts. That had been over two hours ago.

Soon it would be dark, and I was hungry. There was a bowl of fruit on the table in the kitchen; I ate a banana and then, a half hour later, an apple.

The knock on the door startled me. Why was Gunner knocking on his own door?

"What are you doing here?" I asked the man standing on the other side of it.

"I'm taking over your detail," Monk said as he pushed past me.

"Why?"

The reality hit me in the face as hard as I wanted to punch the wall in front of me. Gunner had done exactly what he said he wouldn't do. He'd used intimacy to get me to tell him what he wanted to know, and then as soon as I had, he left.

"I asked you a question," I seethed at Monk. "Why are you here and where the hell is Gunner?"

He walked farther inside without answering me and dropped his bags on the floor near the hallway.

I sat on the bed, cursing the tears that threatened. Gunner had expended a great deal of energy trying to convince me that he wouldn't use intimacy to get me to talk, but that's exactly what he had done. If he did anything to jeopardize my mother's life, I would skin him alive.

What a fool I'd been, thinking he was different. None of them were different. They'd all been trained to get what they wanted by any means possible.

I caught a glimpse of Monk outside on his phone. There had been several ways I'd thought of to kill him. This would be the perfect opportunity to slit his throat, take his phone, and tell the man I was certain he was talking to, exactly what I thought of him.

As though he could feel my threat, Monk turned and made eye contact. Giving him the finger probably wouldn't elicit much of a reaction from him. If only I had a gun. That would make him pay attention. I might even be able to get him to talk.

He nodded, disconnected the call, and walked toward the house. Within seconds, I heard his footfalls coming down the hallway, followed by a knock.

"I've been instructed to give you a briefing."

A briefing? What the hell? I was tempted to tell him to fuck off, but information was my friend. The more I had, the more I could do with it, including getting the hell off this island.

Monk stepped back when I opened the door, and motioned for me to go to the main living area of the house. Once there, he indicated that I should sit. Was he planning to brief me using sign language or did the man ever intend to speak?

I heard what sounded like a printer and then watched Monk leave the room. When he came back, he held several sheets of paper.

"This is for your eyes only," he said, handing them to me.

I looked to my left and right. "Are you saying I shouldn't share it with the animals inhabiting the island?"

"Habit," Monk said, sitting in one of the kitchen chairs.

"Why are you sharing this with me?" I asked after skimming the first page.

"Orders."

"From?"

Monk shook his head, stood, and walked out the front door.

It had been a stupid question. Of course this was from Gunner. I stood and went into the bedroom.

A half hour later, I set the papers on the bed, next to me, and wondered if he'd sent them somehow believing I wouldn't hate him as much if he shared what he and Shiv's team had discovered.

He was wrong. Very wrong. I hated him with every breath I took and every tear I cried over the lying bastard.

23

Gunner

"Where is that *sonuvabitch*?" I murmured under my breath, not expecting Shiv to answer.

Petrov had ghosted, which wasn't a surprise. I didn't care whether we found him or not, as long as he stayed deep enough to leave Raketa alone.

What worried me was that the woman I believed was Raketa's mother was gone too.

My plan had been to get in, get her, and get out. Somewhere in the back of my mind, I knew it wouldn't be that simple.

My guess was that Petrov had made sure Raketa knew her mother was on the compound. It would be easy to get her to do whatever he wanted if he used the woman she'd believed died when she was a child as bait.

Not only was she gone, the compound was empty—seemingly deserted. There was no trace of the arms dealer ever having been here. It was as though the ancient structure had been abandoned centuries ago.

The modern upgrades in the various apartments were the only proof they hadn't been.

"Ready?" Shiv asked, motioning to the corridor that would lead us to the waiting SUV.

Shiv's team had collected what could be used for DNA samples whenever they could find any. I hoped they were able to prove one way or another whether the woman who had been held here was Raketa's mother.

I shook my head. There had to be some clue I was overlooking.

"Where did Alegria say the woman was being kept?"

Shiv pointed to the drawing. "Here."

"I'm going to take another look." I didn't wait for Shiv to argue. I'd take all damn day if I wanted to, and the rest of the team could leave. I'd have no trouble making my way back to the rendezvous point.

"I'll recheck the apartment Raketa was being held in."

I nodded, appreciating that Shiv might also be thinking we'd missed something.

I walked every inch of the apartment, uncertain what I was searching for, but unable to shake the feeling I'd overlooked something.

I ran my hands over the walls, from ceiling to floor and found nothing. I was moving into the kitchen area when Shiv walked in, carrying what looked like an ancient wooden box in his gloved hands.

"What's that?"

"Haven't looked yet."

"Where'd you find it?"

"In here."

I followed him down the corridor, past the apartment Raketa had been in, and into another room that looked as though it might have been used for storage.

"The stone shifted when I walked over it," Shiv said.

I looked at the hole dug into the earth beneath the flooring and was reminded of another op where we'd found documents buried in the floor of a cabin.

"Not very original," I muttered.

"Depending on how old what we find might be, it could be quite original."

"We should do another sweep of all the rooms."

"I agree. I'll have the team move back in."

"You've copied all of it. I'm taking the originals back to Ivashov."

Shiver shook his head. "We've been over this already. Taking the contents of this box *anywhere* is not an option."

"You'll have to kill me to stop me."

He shook his head a second time. "Don't think I haven't considered it. At least wait until the translation is complete."

"There's no need. She'll be able to read what's in it."

With the wooden box under my arm, I left the room. I could hear Shiv cursing me, but I didn't care. I also didn't take him seriously. If MI6 had wanted to stop me, they could've very easily.

I hoped by now that Raketa had digested the information I'd asked Monk to pass on to her. When I returned to the island, she and I would have to craft our next plan of action together.

When I got on the plane that Mantis had waiting on the private airfield near Heathrow, I knew that what I'd expected to be a quiet flight back to the States was going to be anything but, given my three original K19 partners were there, waiting for me.

"What the hell?" I said, unable to hide the smile that gave away how happy I was to see them.

"We figured you probably had your head up your ass over Raketa about as much as we each did over women in the last year," said Razor, hugging me and slapping me on the back.

"Quite a risk leaving Ava," I said, the smile leaving my face.

"If you think my wife doesn't have the full protection of every governmental security agency and a handful of mercenaries, then you don't know me at all."

"Hey, Gunner," said Doc, walking forward to hug me the way Razor had.

"You even got Eighty-eight away from your daughter. I'm stunned."

Mercer walked forward as well, but waited for me to hug him.

"Still scared of me, are ya?" I said, elbowing him in the side.

Mercer laughed. "You think you intimidate me only because I tolerate your delusions."

"I appreciate this," I said, acknowledging each of them.

"Been where you are," said Kade, the man who had initially brought the team together, and who had served as mentor to us all. "Tell us what you've got so far."

I reiterated what they already knew about Petrov's relation to Raketa as well as my belief that the woman who'd also been held at the compound was her mother.

"Pick up any trace of where he might've been headed?" Kade asked.

I had a handful of theories, based mostly on where I knew Petrov wouldn't be welcome. Mainly, anywhere with Russian or Armenian influence. Unfortunately, that still left a long list of possibilities.

"What's in the box?" asked Razor. "This one of yours, Doc?"

Kade shook his head, and so did I. When we believed he'd been killed while deep undercover, we carefully executed the requests he'd made of us, which included instructions for several of what we'd all referred to as "Doc's boxes."

One was to be given to Kade's youngest brother, tasking him with delivering it to the woman that brother was now married to. That wasn't the only thing Kade had left behind. The rest had been up to Mercer to divvy up per our former boss's instructions.

"You'll find out soon enough," I muttered, setting it down on one of the tables. I'd packed the wooden box inside a cardboard one after making sure it was wrapped in acid-free paper and Bubble Wrap. "I'm not opening it again until I get to the island."

I looked toward the cockpit and saw Mantis in place. "What's the holdup?" I asked.

"Mercer and I are staying here for the time being," said Kade. "Razor will travel back with you."

"I thought you were retiring."

"That's the plan. Once this op is complete."

I looked between the two men. "What op?"

Razor laughed and shook his head. "The one where we make sure you get to be the knight in shining armor who rescues the princess, asshole."

I laughed out loud. "There isn't a man alive who is less of a knight than I am, nor a woman less of a princess than my Rocket Girl."

"You have your work cut out for you," Kade said to Razor, picking up his duffel and checking each of his guns before putting them in their various holsters.

"What's that mean?" I asked when no one else reacted.

Razor grasped my shoulder. "It means that I've gotta school you in how to treat a woman between here and Chesapeake Bay."

I shrugged his hand off. "I've handled twice as many women as you have, ol' boy, and did just fine."

"Yeah, that may be true. What you haven't done until now is had any reason to learn how to treat the one woman who will matter more than all the others combined. Notice I said 'treat' not 'handle.' That's your first lesson."

At any other time of my life, I would've given my friend a ration of shit. However, Razor was right. I had realized before I left for Azerbaijan that I'd do anything to keep Raketa by my side for the rest of my life.

"Your second lesson is going to be in groveling," Razor said once Kade and Mercer had deplaned and were on their way to meet Shiver.

I didn't doubt it. Raketa was pissed. I knew that already. However, I'd had good reasons for leaving her behind—five million bucks and an asshole of a daddy. If she was going to be by my side for the rest of my life, I had to keep her alive. Her safety came before whether she was mad or not.

"Monk says she has smoke comin' out of her ears."

"Since when does Monk say anything?"

24

Zary

He was on the island. I knew it without needing to see him or be told. I could feel Gunner Godet's presence. I'd been able to since the very first time I saw him. Monk had disappeared a few minutes ago, although I'd stopped keeping track of him the first day he arrived. I'd never met anyone with a more appropriate code name.

I decided to meet the traitorous wretch head-on, so I went outside and stood near the place where he'd built a fire the night before he left. From there I could see his approach from any direction.

"I brought you a present," he whispered in my ear.

If I had a gun, he'd be dead. Or maybe I would be, considering he'd sneaked up on me without a sound.

Before I could take the swing at him that I intended, he wrapped his arms around me, holding my back to his front.

"You're gonna like it," he said into my ear before kissing the side of my neck.

As much as I tried to stay stiff as a board, continually reminding myself how much I hated him, I was powerless against the assault he was waging on my body with his tongue, lips, and hands.

"I hate you," I said instead.

"I can tell," he murmured as my body relaxed against him.

When I felt the dampness of tears on my cheeks, I pulled out of his grasp and spun around. "You told me you wouldn't use sex against me. You lied to me. *You betrayed me.*"

"I kept you safe. There is no betrayal in wanting to protect someone." When he advanced on me, I took a step backward. "Open your gift before you tell me you hate me again."

I studied the cardboard box he set in front of me. The only thing it could contain that would keep me from hating him was Petrov's ashes. Even then, I'd have to know where my mother was and that she was alive before I could ever trust Gunner again.

"Let's go inside," he said, picking up the package and then putting his other arm around my shoulders.

I shrugged away from him and crossed my arms, wishing I wasn't so curious about what was in the box.

"You're gonna want to do this after you open it," he said, grasping my neck and covering my mouth with his. He nipped at my lip, and I opened to him, hating that I'd missed him as much as I told myself I despised him. My arms wrapped around his neck of their own volition, and I pressed my body against his.

Gunner was the first to let go. "Open it," he said, handing me his pocketknife.

"Where are you going?" I asked when I saw him walk away.

"I'm giving you some privacy."

"Oh." Disappointment was written all over my face; I knew it because of the look on Gunner's as he walked back toward me.

"It's okay, Rocket Girl. I promise this is something you want to do on your own. When you're ready, call my name, and I'll come back out."

Trusting what I saw in his eyes, even through my trepidation, I nodded.

I sliced through the top of the box and saw what was inside was wrapped in what looked like several layers of packing material.

Something morbid occurred to me fleetingly. I might think I'd love it; however, I doubted very much that what was wrapped so carefully was Petrov's severed head.

I shook the thought away as I carefully peeled the layers of plastic and paper.

I hesitated before touching the photographs that sat on top of the box. What if they disappeared or crumbled in my hands? I'd be devastated. My rational self pushed through; there was nothing about them that looked fragile. They had been very well preserved.

If I'd seen the pictures before, I didn't remember. While I didn't recognize myself, I knew the baby, toddler, and little girl in the photos were me.

I did recognize my mother and even my father although he looked nothing like the man who had been holding me captive only a few days ago.

The box held more than photos. There were official-looking documents, cards, and letters—all of which were written in Azeri.

I reached in and pulled out a pair of baby shoes. I guessed they were the same as any other of their kind, but to me, they were precious. Near the bottom of the box, I found a few clothing items and a blanket that felt so soft when I held it against my cheek.

One by one, I opened the cards first, and then the letters. Some had been written by someone I didn't recall ever having heard mentioned. I knew by the signature, though, that they were from my mother's mother. The box also held letters my mother had written in response, all tied in bundles and kept in order by date.

"There is nothing on earth as precious as a mother's love for her child." I read my grandmother's words. "It is boundless and limitless."

When I read my mother's response, I saw that not only had she agreed, but she had gone on and on about how she'd never realized such love existed.

I set the letter aside, rested my head on my folded arms, and cried.

Makar Petrov had not only taken my mother from me, he'd taken love that I didn't remember having away from me too.

I felt Gunner's hand on my back and was grateful he'd come out without me having to ask. I heard him pull a chair closer, and went willingly when he picked me up and held me on his lap.

"Thank you," I murmured and felt him nod.

He held me that way long after the sun had gone down. He stroked my back, kissed my forehead, and kept his arms around me.

There was no way for me to describe the way I was feeling, and I was glad he hadn't asked. The closest I could get was to liken it to someone waking up from amnesia and seeing proof of the life they were just beginning to recall.

"I have something to tell you," he began.

I took a deep breath, sensing what was coming. "Go on."

"Petrov ghosted. There was no sign of him or your mother."

"I see."

There was no reason for me to believe Petrov would kill my mother now after keeping her alive for so many years. I also didn't doubt he'd get word to me before Gunner, or anyone else from K19, MI6, or the CIA found him. He knew that he held the ultimate weapon to get me to do his bidding, and he was right. I'd kill anyone who got in the way of my mother being safe, or I'd die trying.

"He wants his *daughters*," I murmured. "That's what he told me he wanted in exchange for my life."

"You're his daughter too," Gunner whispered.

"Am I?" I wasn't so certain after seeing the photographs. In the few he was in, he seemed to intentionally stand apart from me and my mother. There wasn't a single photo of him holding me. I hadn't read through all of the letters, but I hoped they would provide some clue as to whether my suspicions were correct.

"If you want to know for sure, the answer is readily available, sweetheart."

"I know." A simple DNA comparison, which had likely already been performed, would confirm whether Petrov was my biological father or not. "Do you know?"

Gunner shook his head.

"Thank you."

He pulled his phone out of his pocket and pressed his thumb against the button to unlock it. "Here. Call Shiv."

I didn't take the phone from him.

"Do you want me to do it?"

I rested my head against his chest and nodded.

"Before I do, I want to tell you about Doc and Quinn."

I remembered that the man he referred to as Doc, Kade Butler, and his daughter, Quinn, hadn't known whether he was her father. Ultimately, they found out he was, but the circumstances were so different than mine. Granted, if Kade hadn't been confirmed as Quinn's father, it would've meant that her mother's rapist was.

For me, the proof would simply tell me that I was the spawn of a man I considered the devil, or of a man who'd abandoned my mother once he knew she was pregnant. What good would knowing do me?

"I already know about them," I said when I realized he was waiting for me to say something.

"It's your decision."

I took the phone from his hand and set it on the table. "It doesn't matter."

I looked back at the box longingly, wanting to know more about the life I could hardly remember.

Sensing what I was feeling, Gunner shifted me off his lap.

"I'll give you your privacy back," he said, turning to leave the kitchen.

I rested my hand on his arm. "I'd like it if you stayed."

25

Gunner

I watched as the expressions on her face morphed from happiness to sadness and back again. A feeling I could only describe as pride settled in my chest. Shiv had found the box, but I'd brought it to her. It was the greatest gift I'd ever given anyone.

When she put the last of the letters back in its envelope, she turned to me.

"Thank you."

"You're welcome."

"You were right to tell me not to say I hated you again until after I saw all of this."

"I'm generous that way. I didn't want you to feel guilty." She smiled at my joke, and then the look on her face grew more serious.

"I think I might know where Petrov went."

"Raketa believes that Petrov may have fled to Iran," I told Doc.

"Based on what information?"

"Something she heard about a deal as she was being escorted into Petrov's office."

"Would he be that sloppy?"

"It was the tail end of a conversation and only one word mattered—Azarpassillo."

As soon as she'd said it, I understood where she was headed. The Iranian construction company was controlled by the country's Revolutionary Guard, notorious for greasing the hands of Azerbaijan's wealthiest and most powerful oligarchs.

I knew from the Transparency International Corruption Perceptions Index, Azerbaijan was among the most corrupt nations in the world. A perfect place for the likes of Petrov to operate. However, if he needed to ghost, the Iranians were the most likely to offer him a place to land.

"What about United Russia?" asked Doc.

"I'm not so certain they want him dead."

"We'll work this angle and report back."

I ended the call and looked into Raketa's hopeful eyes. "I think we're on the right track."

She stood and paced the living room. I could almost see the thoughts as she processed them. Raketa wasn't just an assassin; she'd been trained as an operative, and I trusted her instincts.

"I need access to a computer."

I stood, walked over to a locked cabinet, opened it, and handed her a laptop.

"Is it secure?" she asked.

I pulled out a card, inserted it into a slot on the front of the machine, and logged on.

"You're trusting me?" she asked when I turned the computer toward her.

"You're trusting me?" I asked in response.

I watched as she made several attempts at hacking into encrypted Azerbaijani sites. In less than a half hour, she was successful. Most of what she was looking at was in Azeri, although some of the documents were written in Iranian and Russian.

"I've compiled the information you need to send," she told me after more than two hours.

The entire time, I'd sat watching her. She was equally impressive in her espionage skills, ability to quickly decipher what she was reading and determine what was worth passing on, not to mention—hotter than shit.

I shouldn't have been turned on watching a woman sitting in front of a computer, but I was.

"What?"

"Nothing," I answered, willing my body to settle the hell down.

"Gunner?"

I'd stand, but if I did, it would be impossible for her not to know what I was thinking. I looked into her imploring eyes.

"Watching you…"

She folded her arms.

I leaned forward and released them. "Your spy skills make me hot, Rocket Girl."

Her face went from questioning to smiling. She stood and pulled me up with her. "Let's get you cooled off."

"That wasn't what I had in mind."

"I think you know what I meant."

That was another thing about her that never failed to make certain parts of my body twitch. Her accent was sexy as hell too, and even though her English was practically flawless, I could tell when I had her flustered by the way her mastery of the language's nuances slipped.

I couldn't fault her though; it would make me a hypocrite. When she heated my blood, I could barely speak my native language.

"Where are we going?" I asked when she led me out the front door.

"To the waterfall."

"Hang on." I dropped her hand and headed into the bedroom. No way would I forget the condoms this time.

I loved the feel of Raketa's naked body asleep next to mine. That I could stroke her skin, kiss her, even penetrate her body whenever I wanted left me perpetually aroused.

When we came back to the house after our escapades under the waterfall, I couldn't wait to get her back into bed.

"I'm hungry," she'd pouted, making me relent long enough for us to have dinner. The dirty dishes, however, sat in the kitchen.

"Cleanup can wait," I'd said, pulling her into the bedroom.

When she shifted and turned her back to me, I rolled to my side, nestled my front to her back, and wrapped my arm around her waist.

She muttered something indecipherable and appeared to go back to sleep.

In the morning, I'd talk to her about the conversation Razor and I had had on the flight back to the States.

"I don't want to be put in the position of having to lie to Ava," he'd told me. "In fact, I won't do it."

"I wouldn't ask you to."

"They're half sisters."

I knew what Razor was talking about and could even guess what he'd say next. Only moments later, he proved me right.

"They should meet."

"It's up to Raketa."

Razor knew Petrov had asked her to bring Ava and her twin, Aine, to him in Azerbaijan.

I couldn't predict how Raketa would feel about meeting the two women her father considered his daughters when he didn't seem to feel the same way about her.

"Fair enough," Razor had conceded after making me promise to at least bring it up. "I won't say anything to my wife until you've talked to her."

"What are you thinking about?" Raketa asked.

"I thought you were asleep."

She laughed. "You're holding me very tight, Gunner."

I relaxed my arm. "Sorry."

"Tell me why."

"Feeling possessive, I guess."

Raketa turned to face me. "Why?"

I cupped her cheek with my hand. "Because you matter to me, Rocket Girl."

"You matter to me too," she said, bringing her soft lips to mine. "Now tell me why your arm turned to iron."

"Razor and I talked about you on the flight back."

"That's hardly news."

"He wants to arrange a meeting between you, Ava, and Aine."

"I see," she said, her eyes hooding.

"I told him it had to be your decision."

She nodded. "Why does he want this?"

"The main reason is that he doesn't want to have to lie to Ava."

"What do you think?"

"I told you. It's up to you. It isn't something I would've suggested, but I did promise him that I'd at least bring it up."

Raketa turned again so her back was to me. "I'll think about it," she murmured.

I moved her hair so it draped over her shoulder, and kissed my way across her back.

"I can't think when you do that."

"You can think tomorrow," I said, positioning myself so I could enter her from behind. "Are you ready for me, Rocket Girl?" I asked.

She kissed the hand that rested on her arm. "I'm always ready for you, *lyubimaya moya*."

As I joined my body with hers, I hoped she meant the words she'd uttered. There was nothing I wanted more than to be her "love."

26

Zary

As the man I knew I was destined to be with from the day our eyes first met moved inside me, I was overcome by emotion. I'd called him my love because that's what he was. He was the only man who would ever be.

Earlier, under the waterfall, our sex had been frantic, impassioned, hard, and fast. Now, he moved slowly, gently cupping my aching breasts with his hands, and scattering kisses wherever his lips could reach.

Each time we were together was better than the time before. He set every inch of my body on fire with his touch, whether hurried or slow, hard or soft, gentle or rough. I never imagined all the ways he could bring me to the brink of pleasure and then catch me as my body spiraled into a feeling I'd never known existed.

In moments like these, I pushed every lingering doubt out of my head and trusted him.

The realization hit me like a lightning bolt. *I trusted him.* Not just when we were intimate, but always.

"Gunner?" I said when he separated his body from mine after we'd both reached the pinnacle of pleasure.

"Mm-hmm," he hummed between the kisses he continued to rain on me.

"I need you to look at me."

His eyes opened wide and stared into mine.

"I trust you."

He kissed me with a passion closer to that of earlier, under the waterfall, than of our last lovemaking.

He stopped suddenly, his gaze so intense that I almost closed my eyes. I held my breath, waiting, wondering what he was struggling to say.

"Gunner?" I said again.

He brought both hands to the sides of my face. "I love you, Zaryana. I know you don't like me to call you that, but I can't help myself. With me, that's who you are. You aren't the Rocket. You're the woman I love."

"My mother used to call me Zary," I whispered.

"Can I call you Zary?"

I nodded.

"I love you, Zary."

"I love you, Gunner."

27

Gunner

She was quiet the next morning as she watched me make breakfast. Every so often, I'd walk over and kiss her. Each time she'd smile, but soon she'd be lost in thought over something that made her frown. I wondered if it was Razor's request for her to meet Ava. I wished I could reassure her again that whether she did or not was entirely up to her. If that wasn't what was on her mind though, I didn't want to pile another worry on.

I set a plate in front of her that I'd heaped with a vegetable omelet, roasted potatoes, and toast.

"I can't eat all of this," she said, looking apologetic.

I leaned down, kissed her, and smiled. "Whatever you don't finish, I will."

After breakfast I'd planned a vigorous workout—one we both needed not just for our bodies, but for our state of mind too.

"Who taught you to cook?" she asked between mouthfuls.

"My mother. She gave up on Odette, so I was her only hope."

"Your sister doesn't like to cook?"

"Remind you of anyone?" I winked.

When she stuck her tongue out at me, I laughed out loud.

"I like your laugh," she murmured.

"I like yours too."

"I don't laugh. I mean, I do now, but not usually."

"I'm the same way."

"Do you ever wish we could just stay here forever?"

Her question stunned me. "All the time."

"Me too. I can't, though. Not until…"

"Does that mean you'll want to come back?"

I couldn't read the look in her eyes. Was she waiting for me to tell her she could, or that I wanted her to? "I'd love it if you'd stay here with me forever."

"After."

"I understand."

Raketa didn't bring up the conversation we'd had about meeting Ava at all that afternoon, so I didn't either. When she was ready to talk about it, she would.

In the meantime, I was anxiously waiting for word from either Doc or Shiv. We needed to talk about what our plan of action would be.

"We should get ready to leave the island."

Raketa looked startled. "Have they found Petrov?"

"Not yet, but we should be ready to go at a moment's notice. It'll take time for us to arrange transport to Iran if your theory proves correct."

"Do you want to leave now?"

"I don't. I just want to make a plan."

She bit her lower lip and looked away from me.

"Talk to me, Zary."

She turned back and smiled at my use of the name. "Has Doc said anything about UR?"

I shook my head. "Listen, you don't have to go with me. I can have Monk come back, or…"

"She's my mother."

I shifted closer to her on the sofa and put my arm around her shoulders. "I can't read your mind, sweetheart. Tell me what's going on in that beautiful head of yours."

"I'm wondering who they'll send."

"Is there anyone you're more concerned about than others?"

Raketa shrugged.

Knowing that anyone—from UR or Petrov—was on the hunt for Raketa filled me with a sense of dread unlike any I'd felt before. It drove home, in a very direct way, why getting involved with someone else in our line of work was a very bad idea. When it was personal, mistakes came by way of emotion. It occurred to me that Raketa knew this as well as anyone.

"Tell me what happened in Washington."

"Why?"

"How was Topor able to get to you?"

"You know why. You don't need me to say it."

"You couldn't pull the trigger."

"It wasn't because of Petrov."

"I know. It was because he had Ava."

Raketa nodded. "It's only the second time in my life I didn't fire when I should have. Wait, that's wrong. I didn't fire when I was supposed to."

"I appreciate the differentiation."

"I told myself I didn't have a clean shot."

I understood and suddenly wished I *could* force her to stay here, keep her out of harm's way.

"Do you want to meet her?"

Raketa shook her head. "Too dangerous now. Wait until Petrov is dead."

It was three days before I heard from Doc, and then he had nothing new to report.

"He's deep, wherever the hell he is," he said.

"There's no intel at all?"

"Nothing. I've asked Merrigan to get in touch with Rivet to see if there is any other angle she could be working."

"I thought Rivet was retiring."

Sir Ranald "Rivet" Caird was a career British intelligence officer and chief of the Secret Intelligence Service. Doc's wife had once been next in line for his job, but now rumor was that Shiver would be taking over when Riv decided to leave MI6.

"Honestly, I think that's a long way off."

"How's Shiver feel about that?"

"Same as I would if I wasn't ready for a desk job."

That made sense. A man like Shiv would likely never be happy doing anything but work on the ground.

"Keep me posted, Doc."

"You know it."

"Anything?" Raketa asked.

I hadn't realized she was standing right behind me.

"No, but since when are you stealth-girl?"

"I've been watching you."

"Yeah? Think you'll best me?"

"Never, but I'd be happy with number three."

"Not two?"

"You're two."

I put my hand on my heart. "You wound me, woman."

"We both know that you'll never best Shiver."

"That may be right, but you could at least humor me."

Raketa tilted her head like she didn't understand.

"You know, play along to make me feel better about myself."

"I knew what you meant, Gunner."

"So why do you look confused?"

"Not confused. Just thinking."

I waited for her to go on.

"If you trained me, no one would be able to get to me like Topor did."

"Why Topor specifically?"

"I don't know. Just a feeling. Every time Petrov summoned me, he was the one to escort me to his office. Each time, I wondered if that would be when he'd kill me."

I understood. In our line of work, it was essential that we took any feeling, premonition, whatever one wanted to call it, seriously. "Let's get to work, Rocket Girl."

The island was the perfect place for me to mentor Raketa in the same way Shiv had me. It offered a combination of wide-open spaces and concentrated forest. I worked her, day and night, to the point where we ended each session physically spent.

I pulled two troughs from one of the storage buildings, filled one with ice-cold water and the other with warm water.

"I know cold therapy is the rage right now, but I've been practicing contrast therapy for years. We'll do one minute in cold followed by three in warm. We'll repeat this four times," I explained.

"Why?"

"Faster recovery. Reduction in tissue swelling. Decreased inflammation."

Raketa studied me. "Is this really necessary?"

"When you're as old as I am, you'll need it."

She shook her head. "I'm almost as old as you are now, and I don't need it. Maybe you should consider my way is better."

"What's your way?"

"Sex. Followed by twenty minutes in your tub. We'll repeat this four times. At least."

"Yeah, your way sounds much better."

"Better results too."

"See? Much better," Raketa said as she let her body rest against mine in the warm water.

I nuzzled her neck. "You taught me something."

"No, you taught me this too. I have taught you nothing."

"That isn't true. I've learned a lot from you."

"Give me one example."

"I can give you more than one."

She moved away from me and crossed her arms, waiting.

I scrubbed my face with my hand. "This isn't easy for me…" I grabbed her arm when she stood to get out of the tub. "Give me a sec here."

Raketa sat on the edge and refolded her arms.

I looked out the window, up at the ceiling, every-where but at her.

"If you can't—"

"I learned I could love someone, heart and soul, from you," I professed, standing in front of her, naked and exposed, pouring my heart out. "I also learned that I could smile and even laugh, without feeling like I was giving that soul away."

Raketa slid back into the water, pulling me down with her and wrapping her arms around my neck.

"I learned that the mission doesn't always come first and that there are things in life worth taking a step back for. I learned that I would do anything to keep you safe. *Anything.* Including walking away from the only thing I've ever known how to do."

"Anything else?"

"Good Lord, woman. Can you not be sympathetic to how hard it is for me to say shit like this?"

Raketa laughed. "I'm sorry. I would have an equal struggle. I do, in fact."

"Yeah? You have some mushy, flowery, girly stuff you want to say to me?"

She laughed again. "No. Not at all."

"So what's your struggle?"

"There have been…things I've told you that were not easy for me to say."

"I never believed in shit like this."

"You keep using that word. Why?"

"Shit?"

"Yes. Why?"

"I don't know what else to call it. Stuff?"

"That's better than shit."

"As I was saying, I never believed in stuff like this."

"Like what?"

"This kind of love."

"That, I understand. I didn't either."

"I used to think it was a load of…nonsense. Then I watched it happen to men I believed felt the same way I did."

"And you changed your mind?"

"Not exactly. You're responsible for changing my mind."

"What's that?" she asked, hearing the same noise continually repeating.

I jumped out of the tub, grabbed a towel, and rushed from the room.

"We have a code black," said Kade when I returned the phone calls I'd missed.

"Talk to me."

"Sergei Orlov."

"He's dead."

"He's alive."

"*What?* Razor said he was shot between the eyes."

"Evidently, United Russia wanted us to believe he was."

I wondered whether Raketa knew. If she did, wouldn't she be more worried about him than Topor?

"Tell me why Orlov is a code black."

"Shiv received intel that he's headed in Merrigan's direction."

"*Jesus.* Okay, Doc, what can I do?"

"Eighty-eight and I are at least twenty-four hours out, and I don't want to ask Razor to leave Ava."

"You don't need to justify calling on me, Doc."

"What's Raketa's ten-thirteen?"

"She's safe here. Although I'd prefer some backup while I'm gone."

"Done. I'll make arrangements for Striker to head over with Mantis. He'll fly you into BWA, and from there, Onyx will get you to the West Coast."

"Roger that."

"With no leads on Petrov, I'm making arrangements to head back tonight. I'm sorry to pull you over on this but…she and little Laird are my life."

For the first time in my life, I understood how Doc felt. Raketa and I weren't very far along in our relationship, but I still knew it would devastate me if anything happened to her.

"I'll see you in the morning. In the meantime, Merrigan will be safe with me."

"Appreciate it, Gunner. No one other than you, me, and Eighty-eight know why you're headed to Montecito. I'd like to keep it that way."

"Understood."

"That includes Ivashov."

"Roger that." I scrubbed my face with my hand, wondering how Raketa would take the news that I had to leave the island. Would she trust that I couldn't tell her, or would she think I was betraying her again?

"What's happened?"

"There's a situation unrelated to Petrov that I need to take care of. I'll be gone less than forty-eight hours. Striker is on his way here."

"Weren't you talking to Doc just now?"

"Yes, but again, the conversation had nothing to do with Petrov."

She nodded, but I didn't like the look in her eyes. I couldn't ask her again to trust me. She was going to have to process through this on her own. Either she believed me or she didn't, and until I got back from Montecito, there wasn't a damn thing I could do about it except rest assured she'd be safe here on the island.

28

Zary

I waited until I was certain Gunner had left the house and wasn't coming back.

I'd played the dutiful lover and kissed him goodbye, even going as far as telling him to be careful.

With no time to waste, I raced through the house, gathering the bare minimum of what I'd need. I had to get to the opposite side of the property, where the boat delivering Striker would land.

If Gunner thought I was stupid enough to believe that his phone call had nothing to do with Petrov or *my mother*, he was also stupid enough to think I wouldn't have figured out how to get the hell off this island.

After my initial realization that I'd have no one to turn to for help if I had been able to convince Gunner to release me, it dawned on me that there was one place I could go after all—the Armenian Embassy in Washington, DC.

Once I walked through their doors, they'd not only give me asylum, they'd offer up whatever I wanted in exchange for my help getting Petrov. If Gunner thought he was going to get away with going after that evil piece of shit without me, he was about to learn otherwise. I had no intention of letting anyone else take him down. I'd do it myself after I made sure my mother was safe. She was the reason I couldn't trust Gunner or anyone else to handle this op without me.

They may think my mother was insignificant enough that if she died while they were after Petrov, it would only be collateral damage.

No one else could understand that my mother was a link to my past, to who I really was under the armor I wore as an assassin for United Russia. If I lost her again, I wasn't sure my life would be worth living, especially since I now knew I'd never be able to trust Gunner Godet.

29

Gunner

"What the fuck do you mean she's not there? That's impossible. Jesus, Striker, have you looked for her?"

"Screw you, Gunner. Listen to what I'm telling you—I've looked everywhere, and there is no other human being on this island."

Fuck, fuck, fuck. I wanted to rip my hair out. How had she managed to get off?

There was only one possibility, and given how damn smart she was, I could only assume she figured out where the boat bringing Striker to the island would come in, and she'd gotten herself stowed away on it before it headed back to the mainland.

I counted back the time between the boat's arrival and our plane's departure. Add on another thirty minutes, at least, for Striker to determine she was gone, and we were close to ninety minutes.

Raketa had to be at least an hour away from where the boat had docked in Deale.

There was only one place she could go for help, and while she'd admitted to me only a few days prior that she had nowhere, I'd bet she'd figured out the same thing I had.

"Who've you got near Dupont Circle?" I asked Striker.

"Who do you want?"

"Whoever can get to the Armenian Embassy in under fifteen minutes. Once she's inside, we've lost her."

When I saw Striker's name show up on my phone, I already knew we'd been too late. As much as I didn't want to answer, I knew I had to.

"Hey."

"You know why I'm calling."

"Is there anybody on the inside who can get word to her?"

"Negative for now, but Shiv may have someone."

"If he does…"

"Yeah?"

"Never mind."

"Don't give up on her, Gunner."

I had no intention of doing so, not that it was any of Striker's fucking business.

Once Kade arrived in Montecito, I'd track her, and regardless of how powerful an Armenian cavalry she had with her, I'd find her and bring her back where she belonged.

"Good to see you, Doc," I said when my partner walked through the front door of his house and into his wife's arms.

"Where's Orlov?" Merrigan asked.

"I can't answer that." Doc looked over at me. "There's a possibility he was headed to the opposite coast. I'm sorry, Gunner."

Fuck. Orlov hadn't been after Merrigan at all. It was a ruse to get to Raketa. If she were still on the island, I wouldn't be worried. There was no way Orlov could get through the security grid I'd had Striker activate once he and Mantis had left. But Raketa wasn't on the island. If she wasn't on her own, she was being accompanied by a team of Armenians, which essentially amounted to the same thing.

"Shiv should be here any minute, and we'll talk this through."

What I wanted more than anything was to walk out the door of Doc and Merrigan's house and begin the search myself. I didn't want to wait for the MI6 agent to arrive, and I didn't want to talk anything through, but I had to. I had no idea where she was or where she might be headed. For all I knew, she was already in Iran.

The first thing Shiv said when he walked in was how sorry he was about the bad intel on Orlov.

I got right in his face. "I don't give a shit about Orlov. What I want to know is where Ivashov is. Is that something you can help me with or not?"

"Yes."

I was ready to choke him. *"Do I need to keep asking, Shiv? Really?"*

"We know exactly where she is."

"How?"

"Grigor Bedrossian's right hand is MI6."

I felt Doc's hand on my shoulder, and it was a good thing because I was ready to go down Shiv's throat. *"You couldn't have told me that before now?"*

"I have to say I agree with him, Shiv," said Merrigan, coming to stand on the other side of me and putting her arm through mine.

"There were reasons."

"What reasons?" I barked.

"It's no longer a credible threat."

"For fuck's sake," I spat, moving away from Doc and Merrigan. "Just tell me where she is, and I'll be gone."

"Wait," Doc said. "You're not going out on this alone. And if you think you're gonna bully Shiv into telling you where Raketa is, you're wrong. Remember, it's MI6 that knows where she is, Gunner. If you want that information, you'll sit down, shut up, and listen to whatever Shiver wants to tell you. At this point, I doubt it's much."

I pulled a chair away from the table and sat. Doc was right. Shiver had the information I needed, and for some reason, he'd been withholding it.

"I understand that you were able to make the connection between Ivashov and Petrov."

"Raketa is his daughter."

"The woman who Alegria said was also being held by him is her mother."

I nodded.

"Did she tell you why Petrov took her to Azerbaijan?"

"Not exactly."

"Gunner," Doc warned.

"All she told me was that he wanted her to deliver his *daughters*. In exchange for that, he wouldn't turn her over to UR."

"She's his daughter too," said Shiv.

"Glad to hear you're followin' along."

Shiver shook his head. "She had no idea why?"

"Nope, but I sure as hell don't buy that daddy is missing his baby girls."

"Trust funds."

Shiver, Doc, and I all turned and looked at Merrigan.

"It makes sense, doesn't it?" she responded to the unasked question.

It did. When we'd initially determined that Razor's wife, Ava, and her twin sister, Aine's father wasn't Conor McNamara—the identity he'd been living under since before the two girls were born—and was, in fact, Makar Petrov, a black market arms dealer who had been thought dead for the same amount of time, Striker had immediately ensured the agency froze McNamara's assets. I had no idea what the value of the daughters' trust funds might be, but it made sense that, regardless of their worth, Petrov would want to get his hands on as much cash as he could.

"Who's the successor trustee?" I looked at Merrigan, Merrigan looked at Doc, and Doc looked at Shiv.

"You're kidding me, right?" I asked, incredulous that no one had thought of it before now.

Shiver ran one hand through his hair while he made a call with the other.

I sat back in my chair, wishing Shiver would hurry it the hell up. Why did we need to figure all this out now? Every minute Raketa was out there on her own, brought her that much closer to someone else finding her before I did.

"You were on the right track, Gunner," said Shiv, disconnecting the call. "But that isn't the money he's trying to get to."

"What do you mean?"

"An officer of the bank where the trusts reside was named successor agent for Ava's and Aine's trusts. That money is being closely watched by your justice department."

"Get to the fucking point, Shiver," I said through clenched teeth.

"I have my team looking for three other accounts." Shiv looked at Doc. "You should orchestrate the same."

That was why Petrov wanted Raketa in the first place, and why he wanted her to bring Ava and Aine to him. It had nothing to do with him wanting her to abduct his *daughters;* he wanted their money—and hers too.

"You should be looking for four. Or maybe one that has been liquidated recently."

"Svetlana Petrov?" asked Doc.

"Or Ivashov."

Doc walked outside to make the call.

Before I could ask, Shiv handed me a burner phone. "She's in Chicago. There's a plane waiting in Santa Barbara to transport you there."

I took the phone from Shiv's hand.

"You're welcome."

"I would've thanked you if you'd given me the chance."

"I saved you the trouble. I know how much of a hurry you're in."

"Thanks, Shiver. Sincerely."

I was halfway down the block when I realized that I'd walked out without saying goodbye to Doc or Merrigan.

30

Zary

The Armenians never got the credit they deserved. It was as though they'd been expecting me to arrive, and kept the door to the embassy wide open.

I was ushered into the high commissioner's office without as much as a body search.

"Welcome, Ms. Ivashov," he said, motioning for me to take a seat.

"Thank you, Ambassador—"

"Please, call me Grigor."

"I assume you know why I'm here."

He nodded.

"I believe I know where Makar Petrov is hiding."

"Please, tell me what you need."

I didn't need much—money, a cell phone, a computer, and a stockpile of weapons.

He nodded as I spoke, motioning to the various assistants also in the room to collect the items I requested as I outlined my plan.

"We have a team on standby—"

"I work alone. There's only one thing I need to know."

The ambassador nodded.

"Dead or alive?"

He smiled. "Most certainly alive."

A chill went up my spine when I answered the burner phone I got from the embassy and heard a voice say, *"Zaryana."*

I didn't respond.

"If you want to see your precious mama again, you'll follow my instructions very carefully. First, you will tell no one what I tell you, or your mother will die. Do you understand?"

There was no way for me to determine who the voice belonged to; it was being enhanced by a modulator. It sounded like a man, but it could very well be a woman calling. "Yes," I answered.

"Your theory was incorrect. Petrov is not in Iran."

"Where—"

"Silence. You will listen and not ask any questions. I will be in contact again."

"Wait—" I knew there was really no point in trying to stop the person from ending the call.

The only thing I knew for sure was I could no longer operate under the assumption that no one had tracked me yet. More likely, United Russia, Petrov, and K19 knew exactly where I was. That they knew I would only listen and do as they wanted if they used my mother as bait, was more chilling than the phone call itself.

An hour later, I noticed a tail. I wasn't surprised. How good he was, on the other hand, did surprise me. I recognized him from the ambassador's office, but he had to have been trained by another intelligence organization. If I hadn't remembered seeing him, I might think he was with United Russia. Although there was still a chance he was. There were double agents everywhere.

31

Gunner

"Sixty seconds," I heard through the headset.

"Roger that," I answered, already in position. I counted down from fifty-nine and when I got to one, Raketa walked out the back door of the hotel and straight into my waiting arms.

I'd anticipated her struggle, but not the vehemence behind it.

"Settle the hell down," I barked as she tried to scratch my eyes out while hurling a slew of Azeri curse words at me faster than I could translate.

"I don't want to do this, but you're giving me no choice," I said, grabbing her free arm and cuffing them both behind her.

She tried to struggle her way out of my grasp, but she was no match for my strength, particularly in hand-cuffs. When I felt her fight waning, I took her back inside the door she'd come out of, up the service eleva-tor, and to the room MI6 had booked for us.

I opened the door, went inside, and set her down on the bed. "Here we are again, Zary. We have to stop meeting like this."

"Don't call me that," she spat.

"But you told me you liked it. Remember? You were naked in my arms, and we were professing our love for each other. I'm beginning to think you didn't really mean it."

"*You* didn't mean it."

I sat in a chair and pulled it closer to the bed where she sat, reached out, and stroked her face with my finger. "You're wrong. I meant every word I said."

She shifted away from my touch. "Right before you betrayed me for the *second* time."

"I have never betrayed you. The first time, I left you on the island because I believed you'd be safer there. I told you before I left the second time that what I was being called away for had nothing to do with Petrov."

"You lied by admission."

I tilted my head. "Omission?"

"You know what I meant."

"Either way, it wasn't a lie. I was called away on another matter that was of an urgent nature. I specifically told you I would be back within forty-eight hours. Even as I spoke those words, you were planning your departure."

"You lied to me about everything. You told me you wouldn't use sex to get answers from me, but that's exactly what you did. You told me we'd plan together to go after Petrov. Another lie."

"No, Raketa. I didn't do any of those things, and I didn't lie to you. You, on the other hand, lied about trust. You told me you'd never trusted anyone, but I begged you to believe in me, trust me. I understand now why you couldn't."

"Why couldn't I?"

"The entire time, it was I who couldn't trust you. I was just too stupid to see it." I got up and walked to the other side of the room, running my hand through my hair.

It was easy to say things like that out of anger, but I wasn't angry anymore. I was hurt. Way down deep in my soul, I ached, knowing that I'd been right all along. I'd never find love like my partners had. Maybe it was because I didn't deserve it. Maybe if I'd tried harder to get through to Lena, I could've saved her, even if she couldn't have ever loved me the way she'd loved Doc. Maybe living my life without love was my penance for all the horrible things I'd done in my life in the name of freedom and ridding the world of evil.

I walked back and unlocked the handcuffs binding Raketa's wrists.

"If you want to go, I won't stop you. But first, I want you to listen to me."

She shook her arms and then nodded.

"I do love you. I know you don't believe me, but I'm telling the truth. It's the reason I'm here, the reason I wanted to find you, and the reason I want to keep you safe. I can't imagine a world without you in it. I don't want you to have to fight Petrov and United Russia on your own. I want to help you. I want to help you find your mother. That's why I'm here, Raketa."

I turned my back to her. "That's all I had to say. I don't want you to go, but if you do, I won't try to stop you."

I waited a long time after I heard the door of the hotel room close before turning around. I couldn't bear the fact that she'd left without saying a word.

32

Zary

I'd opened and closed the door of the room to see if he really meant he wouldn't try to stop me. And he didn't. I stood perfectly still, barely breathing, waiting for him to turn around and see I was still there. I'd almost gone to him when I saw his shoulders hunch, but I couldn't bring myself to move.

There, before me, was proof that he hadn't lied to me. At least not about everything. He did love me.

It didn't change the fact that, ultimately, I would have to leave. I couldn't risk going against what the voice had demanded of me when whoever it was, clearly knew every move I was making.

"Gunner," I murmured, unable to stand watching his pain a moment longer.

He spun around. "I don't understand. Why are you still here?"

Now that he knew I was, I had no idea what to say. Should I tell him I was sorry, but I still had to leave? He'd given me the opportunity to do so without explanation.

"I…"

He walked toward me.

"Talk to me, Rocket Girl."

"You aren't stupid."

He raised a brow.

"I believed you. When you said you'd help me, I believed you. When you said you loved me, I believed that too. When you left and wouldn't tell me why, I told myself it was all a lie. Everything you said to me. That's the only way I could force myself to leave—by convincing myself you were betraying me."

"I could never. I promise." He reached out and touched the side of my face in the way he always did.

Tears ran down my cheeks as I realized I couldn't make him the same promise. If it came down to choosing between betraying Gunner and saving my mother, I'd betray him in a heartbeat.

"I'm sorry," I whispered. "My mother…"

"Let me help you."

I shook my head as the tears streamed down my cheeks. "I work alone."

"You don't have to. Not anymore. You have me and the rest of the K19 team. You can trust us."

I shook my head again and put my hand on the door-knob. "I can't."

I pulled the door open and was crossing the thresh-old when Gunner put his hand on my arm. "Stay with me. Don't go."

"I wish I could." I pulled away and walked toward the elevator.

"Wait," he shouted. "I know why Petrov wanted you to bring Ava and Aine to him. It's not the reason you think."

"Gunner…"

"You're in the same danger they are. Or maybe it's that they're in the same danger you are. He'll kill all three of you, and I'm sure your mother too, as soon as he gets his hands on what he wants."

I slowly walked back toward him. "You said you'd let me go."

"And I will, but first you need to know what you're up against."

33

Gunner

Was I doing this for the right reasons? I couldn't honestly say one way or the other. All I knew was I couldn't let her leave without telling her everything I'd learned since the last time we were together. I could say it was for her safety, but if I was being honest, it was so I could spend just a few more minutes with her.

Raketa came back inside the room and sat on the edge of the bed where she'd been before. I pulled up the chair and sat as close to her as I could get.

"There are bank accounts that were set up in all three of your names. He's running out of money. That's why he wanted Ava and Aine. I'm convinced that once he gets his hands on it, he will kill you and your half sisters."

"Why did you say you think he'll kill my mother too?"

"There was a fourth account—in her name. It's already been liquidated. I believe her only value to him now is as a means to get you to do what he wants you to do."

"Where are Ava and Aine?"

"Somewhere safe."

Raketa studied me. "You don't trust me enough to tell me."

"It isn't that." Wasn't it? Did I have a valid reason for not telling her where they were? "They're in Oregon. The same place they've been. They're with Razor, and they have a great deal of protection. If we believe their safety has been compromised, they'll be moved. Although at this point, I don't know where that would be."

When the phone in her pocket vibrated, she ignored it, which meant there were things she needed to continue hiding from me.

She stood abruptly. "I have to go."

"I'll say it again. Please. Let me help you."

She shook her head and walked toward the door. "I can't."

Gunfire erupted the second Raketa opened the door. I dove to cover her and pulled her back into the room, firing when I saw the tip of a gun edge at the turn to the elevator.

From what I could tell, there was only one gunman. There was nowhere to go from the corridor the shooter was in but by way of the elevator. There were no rooms, no stairwell.

I eased down the hallway, staying close to the wall, with my gun pointed directly at the corner. I may not be able to hit the person firing, but if I saw the gun again, I'd hit it, and in the moments directly following, I might be able to make the turn fast enough to kill the bastard.

When I heard the elevator ding, I ran forward, reaching the spot where the shooter had been just as the door closed. I pressed the button again and again, and then watched as it descended floor by floor.

Earlier, when I thought Raketa had left, I'd slipped the earpiece of the mic off and set it on the table. I pulled my phone out instead, calling for backup, and then ran back to the room to check on Raketa.

"Where is that *sonuvabitch*?" I seethed to myself when no one answered.

Raketa's eyes were wide when I walked back in the room, her gun leveled at me.

"*Oruzhiye?*"

I nodded.

"He's alive?"

"Yes."

"Iisus Khristos," she muttered, lowering her gun.

"We need to leave. *Now.*"

"There's someone following me. From the embassy, but I think he might be UR."

"He's MI6, but that's not important right now. We have to go."

I led Raketa in the opposite way of the elevator and to the stairwell, calling again for backup.

"Head up," said Striker. In the background, I could hear a chopper.

When we reached the roof, I kicked the door open and held Raketa close as the helicopter landed.

"I thought you were dead," I said when I saw the man flying it.

"I thought you might be too," the man with a distinct English accent responded.

"Raketa, meet Pimm Torosyan."

"We've met," said Raketa.

"Not officially," said Pimm.

"No. Not officially."

"Where are we headed?" I asked once we were in the air.

"We have to make a quick stop to refuel, but I heard you fancy islands."

I smiled. Raketa cringed.

"How does an MI6 agent have access to a safe house in the middle of Lake Michigan?"

Pimm laughed. "It isn't a safe house, and it belongs to my aunt and uncle."

I watched Raketa out of the corner of my eye as she assessed every word Pimm said. She was right to. He was an agent from the UK who had been undercover inside the Armenian Embassy with close access to the ambassador. He could very well be a double or even triple agent.

I'd gone through my own vetting process and was as comfortable with Pimm as I was with Onyx, Dutch, Monk, and Alegria. I was more comfortable with Pimm than Striker, but that was because I couldn't stand the latter. I never could, not from the first day we met. It wasn't that I didn't trust him; I just didn't like the bastard.

"Your team is spread thin," said Pimm. "But you've got plenty of coverage from MI6 until your guys can get here."

"Appreciate it," I said, shaking the man's hand.

Raketa bristled when I put my arm around her shoulders. It didn't surprise me, given the amount of stress she was under. She moved away from my grasp and walked over to the window.

"I can't stay here," I heard her murmur.

"We won't be here long. The important thing was to get you out of Chicago and away from Orlov as quickly as possible."

She nodded, but had a faraway look on her face. I hadn't forgotten that, prior to my gunfight with the Russian assassin, she'd been walking away from me.

"You were leaving."

"I told you I had no choice."

"Actually, you said you couldn't stay."

Raketa shrugged. "There is no difference."

I walked over to where she stood. "There is. Telling me you can't stay means one thing. Saying you have no choice means something entirely different."

"No, it doesn't."

I wasn't about to relent. It absolutely did. Something, or someone, was making her choose to leave rather than stay and let me help her.

"You know it does. Talk to me, Rocket Girl. Tell me who's threatening you and with what?"

I saw the flash of pain she didn't know broke through her steely facade every so often, always over the same subject.

"Someone is using your mother to make sure you work alone."

She didn't react, but I knew I was on the right track. It was the only thing that made sense.

She didn't trust me when she came to me for help initially any more than she did now. Less, actually. Her refusing my or K19's assistance now only meant that she had a very good reason for doing so.

The logical answer was that it was Petrov. Had he been in contact with her? If so, how?

It wasn't a surprise that Orlov had managed to find her. United Russia's resources were far-reaching. Petrov, on the other hand, was operating almost solely on his own. The only help he may have been getting would've been via Azerbaijani or Iranian intelligence, neither of which had the means to effectively track her, K19, or MI6.

"You have the full force of K19 behind you, not to mention MI6."

"I work alone."

"Look at me."

Raketa shook her head, but just barely.

"If I have to, I'll find out who's blackmailing you on my own. Tell me, and you'll save us both time."

"No one is blackmailing me."

"Do you think I can't tell when you're lying to me?"

Raketa spun around on me. "No less than I can tell when you're lying to me."

I'd finally hit on something that she reacted to. I wasn't going to let her slip away from me again. I'd keep her talking as long as I could.

"I've never lied to you. I love you, Zary."

"You think you can play me?" There was a nefarious tone to her laugh.

"I have no reason to play you."

When she turned back toward the window, I stood as close to her as I could without touching her.

"Is it Petrov?"

No reaction.

"You don't know, do you?"

Barely a flinch, but enough that I knew I was right. I put my hand on the small of her back and kneaded her tense flesh. "Let me in, Rocket Girl."

She shook her head slowly, and her eyes filled with tears.

"You've been on your own for too long. You don't have to be anymore. I'm here, and I'll do anything to help you."

"Then, let me go. That's what I need you to do to help me. Let me go, and don't come after me."

"If I asked the same of you, would you do it?"

34

Zary

Would I? When I believed the woman I'd heard while at Petrov's compound was my mother, who had I chosen? Gunner. I could've told him then that I didn't want to go, but I hadn't for the simple reason that I didn't want him killed.

I'd already chosen in my heart, and the realization hit me hard.

"Don't do this," I whispered, wishing I had a way to get through to him, but knowing it was pointless to keep trying.

"I'll never stop. You wanted me; you got me."

I turned my head and caught his smile, but he was right. I had wanted him, more than anything.

Leaving UR was essentially committing suicide, but he was worth it to me.

My mother was different, though. I could make the choice with my own life, but not my mother's. Not now when I knew she was still alive. She was the only person who'd ever loved me unconditionally. I may not remember much about my early childhood, but seeing the photographs that Gunner had brought to me, reminded me that I had once felt loved.

He loved me too, though. As much as I struggled to trust him, when he said the words to me, I knew he wasn't lying.

The phone in my pocket vibrated, and there was no way for me to hide it from Gunner. I was faced with another choice. Did I ignore it or answer in front of him? Both would likely result in my mother's death.

"Hello?"

"You have chosen to ignore my instructions."

"No. I haven't," I responded.

"You have chosen the man over your own flesh and blood. No matter. They'll both be gone soon enough."

"Wait—" I pleaded, but knew it was too late. I'd already heard the beep indicating the call had been disconnected.

35

I heard every word, confirming I'd been right about someone blackmailing Raketa. What I didn't know, and evidently neither did she, was what the blackmailer wanted. That would not be the last time they called, though. Of that I was certain.

Raketa and I had a decision to make. Should we proceed on our own for now, or loop K19 in?

Her eyes were focused on mine, and in them, I saw pleading. I put my hands on her shoulders.

"What is the first thing you know about blackmail?"

She shook her head.

"*Focus.* What's the *first* thing?"

She shook her head again.

"The blackmailer *wants* something."

This time she nodded.

"Second. Blackmailers will target your weakness to get what they want."

"Yes."

She was starting to respond, and instead of despair, I watched the fight come back into her eyes.

"Let's set that aside for a minute and talk about UR. I want you to think really hard about anything you might have on them that we could use to get them to let you go. Anything, Raketa."

"There's nothing," she admitted.

"Keep digging in the recesses of your mind. There's got to be something they want enough that they'll let you go. Start thinking outside the box. What might UR want badly enough that either K19 or MI6 can orchestrate, making sure they get it?"

In my mind, UR's threat against her was more urgent than finding Petrov. Soon, I'd contact Doc and see if he'd come up with anything we could bargain with, but not until I was certain Raketa wasn't going to pull away from me again.

"I know how hard this is for you." I stroked my finger down her cheek and she backed away.

"You haven't had to choose between anything."

"I'm not following."

"You make every decision based on what you think is best. You don't consult me. In fact, you don't consult your team. You lecture me to do something you would never do."

"I don't agree."

She shook her head. "Of course you don't. Here's an example. You told me where my half sisters are only after you had considered whether doing so would jeopardize their safety. You decided it wouldn't, so you told me. If you say you don't weigh everything you tell me first, you're a liar."

Of course I did. I wasn't suggesting I didn't. The point was that I wanted her to accept my help, which meant I was asking her to trust me enough to do so.

"Put your mother's life on the line, Gunner, and then tell me, would you trust me to help you?"

"Orlov found Raketa," I told Doc when Raketa went into one of the bedrooms and asked to be alone.

"I heard. We're sending Striker to the island now. Who else do you want?"

"I'll tell you who I don't want—Striker."

"I know you don't, but listen. If anyone can come up with something on UR, it's him."

"Where's Shiv?"

"You may have forgotten that MI6 doesn't report to me."

"Are you telling me you don't know his twenty?"

"Sorry. Rough night last night. Laird is teething, or going through something else that makes babies turn into screaming banshees."

"Uh, sorry to, uh, hear that." What the hell? Did I really have to hear about Doc's baby? All I wanted to know was where Shiv was. Maybe I should just hang up and call him.

"He's here. Hang on."

I ran my hand through my hair. What happened to the group of badass special ops guys I'd known and worked with for the last few years of my life? Had they all turned into baby-making pussies?

"Gunner."

"Hey, Shiv. Sorry about being such a prick before."

"Enough said. I was giving you a rough time when that's the last thing you needed."

"Appreciate it. I'm sure Pimm told you Orlov found Raketa."

"Who do you think authorized the chopper?"

"Seriously, Shiv? I just apologized."

"Sorry, I was here last night too. I should've left at three in the morning when the little wanker woke me up for the twentieth time. What can I do for you, Gunner?"

"I want Orlov called off, which means I need something big to negotiate with."

Shiver didn't respond, which worried me.

"No," he finally said.

"No, what? No to getting Orlov called off?"

"No, to who you want to use to negotiate with them."

"I'm not following."

"Don't bullshit me, Gunner."

"Shiver, I'm not. I have no idea what you're talking about."

"She's hands off."

My mind raced. Who did Shiver think I was suggesting?

"Not that you could find her."

I decided to see if I could push Shiv into telling me who she was. "Who says she's hands off?"

"I do."

"Give me something more here, Shiv. Why?"

"Because I said so."

There is only one reason that Shiver wouldn't tell me who he was talking about, and that was because it was personal.

"There's gotta be someone else, Shiv. Help me out here."

"If I find out you've pursued this, I'll hunt you down and cut the skin from your body inch by inch."

"Jesus, Whittaker. Enough."

I hung up, unsure of my next move. Shiv was so caught up in whoever it was he was protecting, the conversation wasn't going anywhere.

"Hey, man," said Razor. "I was just about to call you."

"Yeah? What for?"

"You first."

"I just had the strangest conversation with Shiv. We were talking about trying to get UR to give up on Raketa, and he suddenly goes off on how the answer was no to the person I wanted to use to negotiate with them."

"Ah, you played the Kuznetsov card."

"I didn't. And I wish to hell you hadn't given me the name."

"Then, why'd you call me?"

Razor had a point. I did call to see if he had any insight. "You're right. But now that I know she's hands off, I need another name. Got one?"

"Not right off the top of my head, but I'll think on it."

"Who's Kuznetsov to Shiv, anyway?"

"You don't want to go there, my friend."

"Understood. Now, why were you going to call me?"

"I heard about Orlov."

"Yeah, that's why the need to get UR called off has risen to priority number one."

"You need me?"

I was almost speechless. I knew the last thing Razor would want to do was to leave Ava, particularly given the Petrov threat was a priority too, not to mention, she was pregnant.

"I'm good, but I can't tell you how much I appreciate the offer."

"I know the reason Ivashov got off the island was because Doc called you for backup instead of me."

"Flip of a coin."

"It wasn't, and you know it."

I wished to fuck Razor hadn't told me the name of the woman Shiv was protecting. Knowing there was someone UR wanted more than the woman I loved, was a temptation I was having a hard time resisting.

I *couldn't* betray Shiv; he was like a brother to me. Maybe now I understood what Raketa meant more than I'd wanted to admit earlier.

She came out of the bedroom, and we stood face-to-face.

"I can't come up with anything."

I pulled her close and kissed her forehead. "We'll keep trying." All the while, one name, *Kuznetsov,* continued to echo in my head.

36

Zary

I walked down the hallway of the small house, looking for a room where I could be alone. For the time being, I had no way to get off this island, just like I'd had to wait for any opportunity to get off the other one. Once this, whatever it was, was over, I'd never set foot on another island again, particularly one where the only access on or off was by boat or plane.

I lay on the bed, trying to come up with anything that would get UR to let me go. Initially, I believed that K19, with the CIA's backing, would have a strong enough position that they'd be able to negotiate a deal. Obviously, that wasn't happening.

There had to be something UR wanted more than they wanted me dead, but what? What could I deliver that would allow them to save face over my "defection"?

That's what this was about. There wasn't anything I had on them that would hurt their organization. Obviously, UR, the CIA, MI6, and every other intelligence organization in the world executed assassinations when they were deemed necessary. Most, no one ever knew about, outside of the assassin and the person giving them the assignment.

Recently there had been press about former Russian agents living in the UK being poisoned. That was the fault of whoever had been hired to assassinate those agents. If they'd done their job correctly, the deaths would've looked far more accidental. Sure, there'd be plenty, particularly in MI6, who would've known the deaths were assassinations, but proving it to the point that it made the international news circuits would've been impossible.

When Gunner came to tell me that Pimm had brought us food, I went back out into the main room. I knew right away something was on his mind, and whatever it was, was eating away at him.

"Striker should be here within the hour," said Pimm, standing to leave.

"*Fuck,*" Gunner muttered. "I forgot he was on his way."

I knew he didn't like Striker, but that he'd forgotten he was coming added to the mystery of what was distracting him.

"If I was doing what you're doing, you'd tell me to talk to you."

"I'm sorry, what did you say?" he asked, looking up at me.

"Something is troubling you."

Gunner rubbed his shoulder. "It's a damn long list, sweetheart."

"Something specific."

Gunner shook his head, but even that was a lie. I went back to the room I'd been in and slammed the door. More telling than anything, Gunner didn't come after me.

37

Gunner

When Striker came inside without knocking and threw his bag on the floor and said, "I'm here. Let's get to work," I thought long and hard about what the consequences would be if I took out my gun and shot him.

"You don't call the shots," I said instead of killing him.

"For Christ's sake, Paps. Stop with the power trip and tell me why I'm here."

In a split second, I had my hand around Striker's throat and his body slammed up against the wall.

"Gunner?" I heard Raketa say from the hallway.

"Never. Call. Me. That," I seethed under my breath. *"Do you understand me?"*

Striker didn't respond, but I released him anyway.

Raketa stepped forward and put her hand on my arm. Surprisingly, my first instinct wasn't to pull away. She put her hand in mine and led me over to the sofa.

"Can I get you anything?" she asked Striker, who was rubbing his neck.

"A good stiff drink would be nice."

Raketa walked over to the refrigerator and pulled a bottle of vodka out of the freezer. She got three glasses out of the cupboard and brought them to the table near the sofa where I was seated.

"To freedom," she said, meeting my eyes before throwing the shot back. When she sat down next to me, Striker sat in a chair close enough to the table that he could still reach the bottle of vodka.

"You're here to help us figure out how to get UR to let me go without killing me."

Striker poured another glass of vodka, hesitating a moment before pouring another for her and me. "My understanding is that Doc has been working his contacts on your behalf."

"Do you think you'd be here if he'd been successful, you asshole?"

Raketa laughed. "As Gunner said, he hasn't gotten anywhere."

But I had, though. I sat beside her, silent, all the while knowing I had the answer that would save her life. I felt the bile from the shot rise in my throat.

I hadn't had time to look into who Kuznetsov was, but did it matter? Shiv had made it clear that using her as a bargaining chip was out of the question.

If the situations were reversed, would Shiver allow this woman to face assassination when he knew Raketa could be offered in trade? Whether I wanted to acknowledge it or not, I knew the answer.

There were lines that could never be crossed, and at the top was betraying your teammate. While Shiv and I had worked for different organizations the entire time I'd known him, we were still brothers-in-arms.

I studied the woman sitting next to me. Every time I saw her, she took my breath away. Now that I knew how it felt to hold her in my arms, how could I not do everything in my power to save her life?

I wrapped my arm around her shoulders and breathed in the scent of her.

"Is he drunk?" I heard Striker say, giving me one more reason to kill him.

"It's been a very, very long day," Raketa answered. "We should get some rest. There's nothing that can be done tonight."

Striker stood. "Where's my bunk?"

I watched Raketa lead him down the hallway, wondering if she'd just go to bed too. I almost wished she would, not knowing if I could carry on a conversation with her. No matter what I said, the words would drip with the agony I was feeling, knowing I held the answer she sought, but was powerless to give it to her.

"Let's call it a night," she said, walking back to the sofa and holding her hand out to me.

"Go ahead, I'll stay out here for a bit." I brought her hand to my lips. "I'll see you in the morning."

"No, Gunner. There are two beds in this house, and I refuse to sleep with Striker."

"Damn right, you won't," I said, pouring another shot in my glass and throwing it back.

"If you keep going at that rate, you'll be drunk, and I know you'll regret it. If not in the morning, one day you will."

I looked into the eyes of the woman who held my heart. I couldn't sleep next to her, let alone make love to her sweet body, knowing what I did. I could hardly stand to look at her with the guilt I felt.

"I'm going for a walk," I said, pulling away. I went outside, slamming the door behind me.

Never before had I faced a situation like this one. There were good guys and bad guys. Choosing right over wrong was easy. The only time that had come close was when I had to choose Doc's life over Lena's, and even then, the decision had been made for me. In that instance, Lena was evil.

Who was evil in this case? Was Raketa any more or less so than Kuznetsov? I had no idea why UR would want the other woman over her, but either way, there was no way to define either of them as purely good or evil.

When she'd asked me what I'd do if I was forced to choose between her and my mother, I didn't give it any thought. There would never be a time I'd have to.

But now, I was forced to choose between her and my loyalty to Shiver. It wasn't much different than her hypothetical.

I sat on a bench by the water and leaned forward with my arms on my knees. Sitting that way did nothing to assuage the pain in my gut.

Unless I could come up with someone else UR wanted more than *Kuznetsov,* Raketa would be running from them for the rest of her life, and I wasn't sure I could promise that I'd be able to keep her safe.

I heard a door open and close behind me, knowing it was Raketa and wishing it were Striker instead, no matter how much I hated him.

She walked around me, pushed my shoulders back, and sat on my lap.

"Talk to me, Gunner. Let me help you."

I almost smiled at her handing my words back to me, but the pain I felt was too great.

"I can't," I said, wishing I hadn't.

38

Zary

I brought my lips to Gunner's and forced my tongue into his mouth. I circled my arms around his neck and held tight. The only time I saw him in this much pain was when he'd been forced to kill Lena.

I'd refused to take no for an answer that night, and I wouldn't tonight either. I loved him too much to let him deal with his suffering alone, in the same way he wouldn't have been able to let me.

When I pulled back and looked into his eyes, the pain I saw there broke my heart.

"When I got the first phone call, the person used my name, Zaryana. They went on to tell me that if I wanted to see my mother again, I could tell no one about the call or about the instructions I would receive. If I did, she'd die." I took a deep breath. "I didn't get another call until earlier, and you heard the same words I did. Wait, that isn't true. There was another call, but I didn't answer. It was right before I left the room, when Orlov shot at me."

"Why are you telling me this now?"

"Because the only way I know to get you to trust me enough to tell me what's going on, is to trust you first."

"Jesus," I heard him say as he buried his head in my shoulder. I felt his body shake as the dampness of his tears seeped into my sweater.

His arms around my waist tightened as he clung to me and cried. "I don't know what to do," I heard him whisper.

"Tell me, Gunner. What is causing you such pain?"

"I have a name."

I took another deep breath. "Who?"

This was the ultimate test. Would he tell me? If he didn't, I would walk away from him and never look back.

"Kuznetsov."

Now I understood. United Russia had wanted Orina "Losha" Kuznetsov's head since before I'd decided to defect. It was the assignment I'd declined that started the wheels in motion, bringing me to where I was now.

No one declined an assignment from United Russia. Not ever.

I'd waited for a sign, something to happen that I'd know, without question, that it was time to make my move. That was when I contacted Gunner and made the deal with him.

I'd been tracking Petrov from the minute I heard he resurfaced after twenty years. I knew the exact moment the Armenians had taken Aine and two of her friends hostage, and again, the moment they took Ava. By then, Gunner and I were already working on finding Aine.

But it had all started with Kuznetsov.

"That is not an option."

"Why not?" he asked, looking deep into my eyes. "Because of MI6? Because of Shiver?"

I shook my head. "No. This decision is mine alone, not because of anything or anyone else. Because I cannot use Losha to secure my freedom."

"Why not?"

I'd asked for his honesty, would've walked away if he hadn't given it. Now I had to do the same.

"She saved my life. Not just that, she kept me alive, kept me going. She made me Raketa and helped me leave Zaryana behind."

"I see."

"My final assignment from UR, the one I walked away from, was her assassination."

"That's why you wanted to defect."

"No," I said, putting my hands on the sides of his face. "You are the reason I wanted to defect."

Gunner's eyes bored into mine.

"I knew from the first time I saw you that one day I would be with you."

Gunner nodded. "I felt it too."

"Come inside with me," I said, standing and taking his hand. "Let's pretend we're back on your island where nothing can touch us. Where we can be free to love each other without fear for our lives."

39

Gunner

I couldn't have predicted it would be different, but it was. Holding Raketa in my arms after sharing so much of ourselves, trusting each other with the things that were ripping away at our souls, had freed us to simply experience love.

Our touch was tender and slow. Where passion drove us before, this time, love took the wheel. I didn't know what tomorrow would bring, or how we would get Raketa out from under United Russia's threat, or how we would find Petrov and emancipate her mother, but together, we would.

"It's about damn time you surfaced," Striker said when I walked in the kitchen. I responded by flipping him off.

"Where's Raketa?"

"Still in bed."

"You let her stay there alone?"

I spun around from the coffeemaker. "You don't get to think about her in bed. In fact, don't say another word about her. Not even her name."

"That'll make it tough for me to give you the solution to her problem."

"Don't dick with me."

"Since you are, essentially, my boss, I'll go ahead and tell you how the woman whose name I am forbidden to mention can get United Russia to let her go."

"If you're going to suggest Kuznetsov as a bargaining chip, forget it. She won't go for it, and neither will I."

"Not to mention that Whittaker would skin me alive."

I would think about why everyone but me seemed to know about Shiv and this woman later.

"Get to the point."

"I'd rather wait for…you know who. She was the one who made me think of it in the first place."

Did this man not realize how much closer he came to death with every word he spoke?

I growled in his direction and went back down the hallway to rouse Raketa.

"Good morning," she said, stretching her arms over her head, causing her nipples to pop out from under the sheet. I couldn't help myself from taking a taste.

She ran her fingers through my hair. "I am in a surprisingly good mood today, considering I have a five-million-dollar bounty on my head and, in addition to that, my own father wants to kill me."

"About that. The asshole in the kitchen says he has a solution. Something he said you made him think of in the first place."

"I'm intrigued."

"By the way, I made sure he wasn't going to suggest Kuznetsov."

The smile left Raketa's face, but she didn't look sad. "I love you so much, Gunner."

I covered her mouth with mine, demanding my tongue's entry, and kissed her hard. "So much" didn't scratch the surface of the depth of my feelings for her.

I broke away from our kiss and pulled her from the bed. "Put this on," I said, tossing her a robe.

"Does every house on every island in America come with one of these?" she asked as she tightened the robe's belt around her waist.

"Azarpassillo," Striker said when Raketa and I walked into the kitchen.

"What about it?" I asked, remembering she'd mentioned the same thing.

"There's your answer."

"Explain," I said.

"You don't think United Russia wants that money flowing their way instead of Petrov's? We're talking billions of dollars. Why do you think Petrov is so anxious to get his hands on her money?"

"He has to prove to the Iranians he has enough capital to get the deal done," muttered Raketa.

"Exactly," said Striker. "Typical Ponzi scheme."

I poured her a cup of coffee and handed it to her. "So, we do what exactly?"

"Put the deal together. It's gotta be worth a hundred billion at least. What are they offering for this one's head? Five mil? It's easy math. A hundred bil to let five mil go."

Raketa looked at me and laughed.

"What?"

"The look on your face."

I shook my head and turned back to Striker. "What else?"

"There'll be a second part to this deal."

"What's that, Striker?" Raketa asked.

"Petrov."

"What about him?"

"That UR hands over his head on a stick."

"Who works the deal?"

"Me."

"Get your shit together and then arrange to get us a ride," I told him.

"Where are you going?" Striker asked.

"*We're* goin' to Montecito to meet with the rest of the team."

"That means you think it'll work."

I rested the palms of my hands on the table in front of Striker. "Don't you?"

"Of course I do."

"Then, shut up and get moving."

Raketa stood behind me and put her arms around my waist when Striker left the room.

"He wants your approval so badly."

"Tell you what, Rocket Girl, he puts this deal together, and I may end up likin' him."

"There's one more thing."

"Say it."

"My mother. I want her ensured safety written into this deal. Not just her. Ava and Aine too. We walk away without a scratch and with the promise that we'll never hear from UR again."

"That seems like a reasonable request."

"Does it?"

"I'd say a hundred billion dollars might be worth some concessions."

"Do you think Striker can make this happen?"

I lowered my voice. "Not alone. That's why we're powwowing."

I could feel Raketa's body trembling next to mine, but doubted she was nervous about facing the full force of the K19 team. If I was being honest, I was jittery from the time we left Pimm's family's house until we drove through the gates of Doc's compound. Even then, I knew I'd feel a lot better once we were inside and got this deal rolling.

I'd studied Striker on our way here, looking for signs of self-doubt, but the bastard was as cocky and annoying as ever. The CIA was probably glad to see him go when he resigned to join K19.

"Come in," Merrigan said, holding baby Laird in her arms. I hoped he didn't start wailing during the meeting; there was something about babies crying that worked my last nerve worse than Striker did.

Raketa fawned over the baby while I surveyed the room. Everyone was here.

Mantis and Pimm had flown them in. Mantis took a seat on the other side of the room rather than the empty one next to Alegria. Onyx was on his co-pilot's right while Dutch and Monk were head-to-head over something, and Eighty-eight was walking out of the kitchen with a cup of coffee. Neither Shiv nor anyone else from MI6 other than Pimm was here, which puzzled me. Shouldn't they be privy to this deal?

I approached Razor, who was looking at his phone.

"Good to see you too," I said when Razor looked up but his expression didn't change.

"Sorry, man. You probably aren't gonna feel that way when you find out Ava and Aine are here with me."

Given everyone but the contractors K19 kept on the payroll was here, it didn't come as a surprise that Razor brought his wife and sister-in-law with him. I hoped that Raketa realized the same thing.

"What about their mother?"

"Here too. So is Quinn."

I nodded, my eyes meeting Raketa's from across the room. "Where are they?"

"Upstairs."

"Roger that," I said, walking to where Raketa stood. "Come with me for a minute." I took her hand and led her out of the main room and into the kitchen.

"Your half sisters are here," I told her once we were out of earshot of the rest of the group.

She nodded. "I expected they might be."

"They're upstairs along with their mother."

Raketa took a deep breath.

"You're under no obligation to meet them today. I'll understand if it's too much. So will they, along with everyone else."

She nodded and leaned forward so her head rested on my chest. "I don't know what to do," she whispered.

I put my arm around her, loving that she was confiding in me.

"Let's get through this meeting and then see how you feel."

When we went back to the main room, Shiv was walking through the front door. I made eye contact with him, and Shiver acknowledged me with a head nod.

I felt as though something was off between us and hoped we'd have a chance to talk privately later.

I bristled when another man, one I didn't recognize, came through the front door.

"Who's that?" I asked Razor.

"Striker's replacement at the company."

"How come we haven't met him until now?"

"Not sure."

"What have you got on him?"

Razor rattled off the guy's credentials like he was reading them from a list, the way he usually did.

"Kellen McTiernan. Age thirty-three. More of a thinker than doer, but with an astronomical IQ. Huge into traffic and signal analysis."

"Isn't that more NSA?"

"Yeah, but that's how smart he is. Evidently, they fought hard for him over at the fort, but the company already had him."

"Code name?"

"Money."

"Striker called him in?"

"I heard it was higher level."

That made me feel better. Evidently, someone at CIA headquarters thought this deal was worth making, so they sent someone in who could work the numbers.

"Let's get started," said Doc, motioning to the empty seats. Raketa and I remained standing while McTiernan was introduced to the group.

The man didn't say much, but took everything in when Striker outlined "his" plan.

"Doc and Fatale have the strongest relationship with United Russia, but I'm proposing Gunner and Shiv take the deal to them."

Huh? What the hell? Striker hadn't said anything about me taking a deal to UR. "Why?" I asked.

"Because the two of you want this deal more than anyone else."

That had to mean Kuznetsov was being included in the package. I shook my head. Was a hundred billion worth the lives of *two* of UR's most wanted?

"I'm not a deal-maker," I said, making eye contact for the second time with Shiver.

"Yeah, but you'll scare the shit outta them," Razor quipped.

"I don't like it." I looked to Doc for support.

"I'm with Striker on this," he said, answering my unasked plea.

The expression I saw when I looked at Raketa told me she agreed with Doc and Striker. Later, when we could talk privately, I'd find out why.

Shiver stood and paced behind one of the leather sofas. "It'll require financial acumen that may be above either of our pay grades," he said, smiling at me.

"Take McTiernan with you," Doc suggested. "He's got OFAC credentials."

Who was this guy? What Razor said he did sounded like NSA, he was here with the CIA, and now Doc was saying he'd worked with the Office of Foreign Assets Control? How had he not been on our radar? If there was anyone I would propose as a K19 partner, it would be this guy.

"I have something to add," said the guy I was studying.

"Go ahead."

"There's another piece to this puzzle that will likely mean the deal will be easier to make."

"And what's that?" I asked. Why didn't people just say what they had to say instead of wasting time setting it up?

"United Russia approached Azarpassillo first."

Was I dreaming? This was almost too good to be true. "Why the hell isn't Petrov at the bottom of the Caspian Sea for real this time?"

"I can answer that," said Shiv. "They're working on it. We aren't the only ones hunting him."

That wasn't good news. My eyes met Raketa's. "We need to find him first."

If they got to Petrov first, UR wouldn't have any reason to agree to even meet. They'd be able to negotiate the deal with Azarpassillo on their own.

When Raketa's burner phone vibrated in her pocket, all eyes landed on her. She looked at me imploringly.

"This way," I said, leading her through the sliding glass door of the kitchen and out to the patio.

"Yes?" she answered.

"Devochka moya, Devochka moya," said her mother's unmodulated voice.

Raketa gasped. "Mama?" she asked with an accent more pronounced than I was used to hearing.

I couldn't decipher what Raketa's mother said next, but distinctly heard, "Top—" and then the call abruptly disconnected.

"Tell me what she said."

"She was so emotional, it was difficult to understand her," Raketa told me with tears in her eyes. "But do you think she was about to say Topor?"

That was the first thing I thought, but she could've been saying anything.

"He hates me," Raketa whispered.

"He works for Petrov."

"It seemed like more than that. I got the feeling he would've killed me, given the opportunity."

"You'll hear from him again, whether it's Topor or Petrov himself, and now you know exactly what he wants."

"In the previous call, he said he'd kill her."

"If I remember what you told me correctly, he said something about if you ever wanted to see her again. Semantics maybe, but they could also mean two different things."

"You do that a lot."

"What's that?"

"Focus on the actual words said instead of assuming their meaning."

"It's important, Raketa. Especially in our line of work."

"I'm not good at recognizing the difference."

I pulled her close. "There's a lot I'm not good at. That's why we're a good team."

"We have to find Petrov."

"Yes, we do. Let's go back inside and see if they've made any headway with a plan of action."

"Where's Shiv?" I asked.

"Upstairs with Eighty-eight," said Doc. "There's a viable lead on Petrov's whereabouts."

"Iran?"

Doc shook his head. "Oregon."

Fuck. On the other hand, Ava and Aine were here in California. If Petrov really was there, he was unaware of their whereabouts.

Raketa tugged at my sleeve and handed me the burner phone.

Manzanita, said the text that came through.

"It's like he can hear us," Raketa whispered.

"Doc?" I said.

"What?"

I made a sweeping motion over her body. Rookie mistake, and one Razor had made with Ava. When it seemed like Petrov knew where she was within minutes of her arriving there, it finally dawned on my teammate that they'd never swept her suitcase for a tracking device. Sure enough, that's where we found it. I *had* swept her belongings, but not Raketa herself.

I put my finger in front of my lips and motioned for her to follow me inside. If her premonition was correct, our entire mission was compromised because Petrov knew exactly what we were about to do.

Something was bothering me about the phone calls. If Petrov was desperate to get his hands on her money as well as Ava's and Aine's, why wasn't he baiting her in a more direct manner? Instead of disconnecting the call, why hadn't he told her he'd kill her mother if she didn't come to wherever he was and bring her half sisters with her? If his intention was to kill the three of them, which I figured was the most likely outcome, he would want them together.

Was that what the text was about? Was he telling her he was in Manzanita so she'd just show up? That didn't make sense.

I followed as Doc led Raketa into one of the downstairs bedrooms. "I'm sorry," I said as I turned on the device that would let us know if she was carrying a bug on her clothing.

I'd gotten just below her shoulders when the device went off. Something had been planted in her sweater. It probably tracked her location as well as picked up dialogue. It was almost too easy to find it.

Wait. The sweater she was wearing had come from my sister. The only way someone could've planted something in it would've been on my island, or, possibly in between the time she left and the time we met up in Chicago.

My thoughts filled me with rage. It was so fucking obvious. I stormed out of the bedroom and slammed the door closed behind me.

"Where's Pimm?" I asked the group still sitting in the main room of the house.

Each of them either shrugged or said they didn't know. I stormed upstairs, but Pimm wasn't with Shiv and Eighty-eight either. As I was headed back downstairs, something caught my eye through the window in the stairwell.

Pimm was outside on this phone.

I stalked downstairs and out the door. I didn't bother to grab my gun from the holster; I was going to rip the man apart with my bare hands.

"What the—" Pimm eeked out before my fist came in contact with his face. I didn't stop with a single punch; I kept going, landing blow after blow on the man's body.

Somewhere in the back of my mind, I heard shouting, but I didn't stop.

"Gunner!" Razor yelled, grabbing me from behind while Doc and Shiv picked Pimm up and moved him far enough away that I couldn't reach him if I escaped Razor's grip.

"What the fuck are you doing?" Razor screamed at me while I stared at the bloody pulp of the man with a burning hatred.

"He bugged her." I looked up at Shiv. *"Your man is a goddamn double agent, you fucking asshole."*

"You're wrong, Godet," said Shiv, his voice too calm for me.

"Fucking liars. Both of you."

"He isn't lying," said Doc. "It isn't in her clothes."

"What?"

It took me a minute to process Doc's words. What was he saying? When I realized what my teammate meant, a roar hurled from my chest, through my body, and out of my mouth. Someone had planted a tracking device *inside* Raketa's body. It could've been anyone, but more than likely, United Russia had done it years ago.

"I know what you're thinking," said Razor, his hands gripping my shoulders while I tried to catch my breath. "If it was UR, they would've killed her the minute she left Moscow. They wouldn't have wasted time sending Orlov."

"Who?"

"Petrov."

That didn't make sense either, not that I could get my brain to process rational thinking. I looked at the man who I'd nearly beaten to death and fell to my knees.

"Jesus, help me, I'm sorry," I practically wailed. I looked between Doc and Shiv, and instead of recrimination in their eyes, I saw pity. I'd killed a lot of people in the course of my life, but I'd never lost control like I had today. I'd never felt that kind of rage. How many times had I hit Pimm before Razor stopped me? Ten? More?

"Is…he…"

"There's a bus on the way."

"I'll go with him."

"No. You won't," said Doc.

"Whatever he needs…God, Pimm…I'm sorry." I didn't know whether the man could hear me, whether he was even conscious.

"Raketa will need you to be with her."

"Right," I said, studying the wounds on my hands. "Shiv?"

"Save it, Godet. I don't want to hear a bloody thing you have to say."

I heard the sound of the ambulance sirens getting closer, and watched as it pulled through the gates of Doc's compound. Two paramedics lifted Pimm onto a stretcher and loaded him into the back of the vehicle. Shiv climbed in with him, and the doors closed.

"What have I done?" I said to Razor as we watched the ambulance pull back out of the gates of the compound and speed away.

"Nothing I wouldn't have done."

"Don't say that. You wouldn't have—"

"Yeah, Gunner, I would've. Doc and Eighty-eight would've too."

I didn't know why my friend was telling me this. I knew it wasn't true. I'd never seen any of them lose control that way.

"It doesn't make it right," said Doc, coming to kneel beside me, "but Razor's right. If I thought someone had planted a device inside my wife, and that person was standing in front of me, I would've killed him. I wouldn't have just hit him; that would take too long. I would've snapped his neck, and I wouldn't have asked any questions."

I hung my head, more ashamed than I'd ever been before in my life. "Where's Raketa?" I asked, not sure I really wanted to know.

"I'm here," she said, walking toward me.

Both Razor and Doc stood and went inside when she fell to the ground beside me.

I leaned into her and cried. I couldn't speak. I couldn't tell her how sorry I was, or how ashamed, or any of the horrible thoughts flying through my head faster than I could process them.

She just held me, rocking my body with hers as I cried. "I could've killed him."

"That's how much you love me," she murmured.

I didn't understand her reaction any more than I could Razor's or Doc's. The only person whose actions seemed logical was Shiv's. I had no idea what would happen with the op now, except I wouldn't be a part of it.

"Come inside now," said Doc to us. When I stood, Raketa wrapped her arms around me.

We walked through the front door and followed Doc back into the bedroom we'd been in before.

No one spoke as Raketa lay on the bed and Doc prepped the area under her arm. As a physician's assistant, he had the experience to remove the device that had likely been planted very close to the surface of her skin. He motioned me to the other side of the bed where he showed me the tiny scar that looked like she might've cut herself shaving. It was healed to the point where it would've been difficult to see unless someone was looking for it.

I held Raketa's hand and closed my eyes as Doc made the slight cut and removed the microscopic device. He used tiny forceps to set it on a sterile pad. In the next few minutes, Eighty-eight would dismantle it under a microscope and look for clues that would lead us to whoever made it.

The rage I'd felt earlier rolled inside of me, and I did my best to tamp it down. Even if Petrov, or whoever had done this to her, were standing in front of me, I couldn't lose control the way I had again.

"It'll sting for a while," Doc said when Eighty-eight took the device and closed the door behind him.

"Thank you," said Raketa, acting as though the pain didn't faze her.

Doc left the room too, leaving us alone.

"I didn't trust him either," she murmured. "I was sure he was working for UR."

"Pimm?"

Raketa nodded.

What I'd accused Pimm of doing was planting a device in her clothing. That alone had sent me into a rage. But that hadn't been true, which meant the person who had implanted it in her body was still out there. Soon they'd know the device had been removed. What would happen then?

As if on cue, the burner phone vibrated. We both looked at the screen when she pulled it out of her pocket. It wasn't a text; it was another call.

40

Zary

I answered without speaking. The voice was modulated, like it had been before.

"You have killed your mother, your sisters, your boyfriend, and yourself. Stupid, stupid girl. I can no longer protect you."

Gunner's look of shock mirrored my own when the call disconnected.

"Protect me? It has to be Petrov."

"What makes you so certain?" Gunner asked.

"The last time I saw him, he said something similar. 'You're here for your own protection.'"

Gunner nodded, but he didn't look convinced.

"Talk to me," I said, using the words he said to me so often.

"Why would he say you've killed your mother, et cetera? Wouldn't that warn you away?"

"He also called me 'girl.'"

"Is that significant?"

"I was in his office, telling him about Topor walking into the apartment where they kept me, whenever he felt like it. When I hesitated, he called me 'girl.'"

Gunner still didn't look convinced, and the more I told him, the less I believed it myself.

"What should we do?"

"I'll talk to Doc."

41

Gunner

"Got a minute?" I asked Doc, who was sitting on one of the sofas, seemingly staring at nothing. No one else was around. I wondered where they'd all gone, but now wasn't the time to ask.

Doc nodded and motioned for me to sit down.

"I know I fucked everything up today, but there's still an op that needs to be carried out. At least I hope there is."

"Nothing has changed, Gunner."

"How's Pimm?"

"You're not quite as deadly as you seem to think. He needed a handful of stitches, but you didn't do any permanent damage."

"Maybe not to his body…" I mumbled.

"There isn't a man on our team who hasn't been where you were this afternoon. The difference is to what degree. You and Pimm will figure this out. Maybe not right away, but eventually."

"What about Shiv?"

"He's pissed, but he's also operating under the same stresses you are."

"Kuznetsov? How come I'm the only one who knew nothing about her?"

"You aren't, and it was by design. The bounty on her head is twice that of Raketa's."

"She wouldn't give her up."

Doc nodded, as though the news wasn't a surprise.

"Do you believe Petrov is in Manzanita?" I asked.

"Could be a trap."

"She got another call."

I told him, word for word, what the caller said. Before I finished, Doc had a theory.

"How much do you know about Evasov?"

"Onyx and Monk are putting together a file as we speak."

"What about Razor?"

"What about me?" he asked, coming downstairs with Ava behind him.

I stood and walked over to her. "Long time, no see," I said. I'd always have a soft spot in my heart for Razor's wife, and by the look on her face, she felt the same way.

"I heard you had a rough day."

"Pimm did. I didn't."

Ava led me back over to the sofa and sat down next to me. "I know you better than that, Gunner."

"To be honest, I've never felt more ashamed." The words were meant for Ava's ears only, but I'd make the same confession to Doc and Razor.

"What do you want to eat, Avarie?" Razor asked from the doorway to the kitchen.

"Pancakes. Pizza. Pasta." She rubbed her belly. "This little nugget likes carbs."

"I'm happy for you," I told her.

"I know you are. I've missed you."

"What do you think your mom and Aine would like?" Razor hollered.

"They're fine with whatever I want." Ava moved closer to me. "How's Raketa?" she whispered.

"Stressed. Scared."

Ava nodded. "I'd really like to meet her."

I hadn't realized until right now how much the two women looked alike. Raketa was more petite than Ava, who took after her mother, but there were enough similarities that I might guess they were related even if I didn't know for sure.

"She wants to keep you safe."

"But we're both here, and so is Aine."

"It isn't my decision, sweetheart."

"I know. I just—"

"Hi."

I looked up and saw Raketa in the doorway.

"Hi," said Ava, standing.

I could see Razor in the kitchen, behind Raketa, watching like I was.

Raketa came farther into the room; Ava met her halfway.

"I feel like I should thank you," said Ava.

"What for?"

Ava smiled. "From what I've heard, you saved my life. Aine's too."

"I don't really think so…" Raketa's eyes met mine. She was way out of her element. That was evident.

"I know Aine would really like to meet you too."

"I…I…um…that would be nice."

"I'll go get her. I'll spare you Peggy, though. I think she's napping anyway."

"You don't have to do this," I said when I was certain Ava was out of earshot.

"I do now," she snapped. "I'm sorry. I shouldn't have come in here. I thought I could, but…"

"Come on. We'll go for a walk."

I took her hand and led her outside.

"Talk to me, Rocket Girl."

She smiled.

"I'm not her sister."

"No. You're not. You share DNA."

"That's the way I've always thought of it, at least in the last few months. I'm not anybody's *sister*. Whatever she's looking for…I don't know how to give her."

"Two things. First, I don't know that Ava is looking for you to give her anything. Second, you said you don't know how to give it to her. Does that mean you want to learn?"

Raketa didn't answer right away. She walked through the garden, stopping every so often to smell the flowers.

"Things grow year-round in California. Nothing grows in Moscow."

I nodded, waiting to see where she was going with this.

"She cannot understand the life I've led."

"There is no reason for you to share that with her."

"But she will ask."

I shook my head. "She's married to Razor. Not asking is part of her everyday life."

"And if she does?"

I walked closer and put my arms around her waist. "Tell her it's something you don't want to talk about."

Raketa rolled her eyes.

"If that is your only fear, it's unwarranted."

She cocked her head. "What do you mean?"

"You have no reason to be concerned."

"What about the sister?"

"She's no different. In fact, Aine is the quieter of the two."

"No," she said, shaking her head.

"You aren't the only one who's had a difficult life, Rocket Girl. Petrov is their father too."

"They grew up with him. Did he beat them?"

She already knew the answer to that question. "They rarely saw him, or their mother. Like you, they were alone. Shipped off to boarding school." I looked up at the house. "You know all this, Raketa. If you aren't interested in learning more or spending time with them, you don't have to justify it to me."

"I don't."

"Not a problem. I mean that."

I heard the front door open and was relieved to see Doc walking toward us rather than the twins.

"It's set. You, Shiv, and McTiernan will meet with UR the day after tomorrow."

"Where?"

"Los Angeles."

Raketa put her arm through mine.

"You'll be safer here."

She shook her head.

"Do they know what we're after?"

"Affirmative. And they know what we're offering."

"Give us a minute?" I asked.

"Take all the time you need. I believe Razor is making arrangements to take Ava, her sister, and their mother to the house in Cambria."

"Roger that." It wasn't fair that everyone had descended on Doc and Merrigan, particularly with the baby. There were two houses less than three hours from Montecito where most everyone could stay, depending on which of the partners were needed elsewhere. I wasn't aware of any other ops going on, but that didn't mean there weren't any.

"Raketa and I can stay up there too," I said.

"Who do you want with you?"

"What are my choices?"

Doc laughed. "Razor is off the table, and so is Pimm. Otherwise, you have your pick."

"Mantis and Alegria."

Doc frowned.

"What?"

"Not a good idea."

"Okay, so much for having my pick. Onyx and Alegria."

"Good. I'll set it up. Monk and Dutch will go with Razor. Striker and Mantis will set up in the Harmony house, and Mercer and Quinn can go home. That everybody?"

"McTiernan."

"Right. He'll go with Striker and Mantis."

"That just leaves Shiv."

"He'll stay here with us."

I raised a brow.

"What?"

"Nothin'."

"He can buy a damn pair of earplugs." Doc turned to Raketa. "Sorry, you two wanted to talk."

"Where are we going?" she asked when Doc walked away.

"We have a place in Cambria. Not too far from here. We'll head there tonight."

"And so will Razor?"

"Two houses, sweetheart, and we'll take separate cars."

She nodded.

"It'll be okay. In forty-eight hours, the deal will be made with United Russia and Azarpassillo, securing your freedom. Before Petrov can get wind of it, we'll go after him. It's almost over."

"I hope you're right."

So did I, because right now, even I had a hard time believing what I'd just said.

"Hey, Raze. What do you know about Topor Evasov?"

"Not a lot more than you do. He was thought to have been executed by Azerbaijan's military as part of that mass wave of arrests made last year."

"That's right, he's Armenian. A double agent."

"There's a theory that he secretly ran everything in Azerbaijan for Petrov when he was living as Conor McNamara. Couldn't have done it alone, though."

"What else?"

"Late forties. Cut his chops in the Armenian National Security Service."

"So Petrov turned him?"

"Yeah, probably."

I knew Razor almost better than I knew myself. Something was on his mind, and whatever it was, Razor was piecing it together on the fly.

"Tell me again what the mystery caller said."

I reiterated every word.

"That last part…'I can no longer protect you.'"

"It's odd. That's what made Raketa think it was Petrov. While she was at his compound, he told her she was there for her protection."

"I can no longer protect you."

"What are you getting at, Raze?"

"But he was able to protect her when the chip was still implanted."

I was usually able to be patient when Razor was thinking out loud. Not this time. "Get to the point."

When Razor opened his laptop, I sat down.

"Where's Raketa?" he asked, but I didn't answer. I knew Razor was too lost in what he was doing to hear my answer anyway.

Earlier, when Raketa and I had come back inside, she'd asked if I'd mind if she talked to Ava alone for a few minutes. I wanted to ask why since she'd just told me she didn't want to, but I'd let it go and went in search of Razor.

"I had a feeling…"

"Jesus," I growled. *"What? Get to the damn point!"*

"Ivashov, Evasov."

"Both common Eastern European names."

"Not so much."

"Raze, I love ya like a brother, but if you don't get to the point, I'll…"

Razor looked up at me.

"Never mind. I'm not in a position to make threats, even if I'm not serious."

"Take it easy on yourself, Gunner. You've never seen my bat-shit crazy."

"If I haven't, has anybody?"

Razor shrugged. "No, but…"

"I changed my mind, if you don't tell me where you're going with this in the next ten seconds, I'll rip your face off."

"Svetlana Ivashov is Armenian."

"But Petrov isn't?"

"Nope. Azerbaijani all the way."

"He had to know his wife's nationality before he married her."

"We need some inside intel on this. Too bad Pimm… sorry, man."

"What are you getting at?" I asked, my voice low.

"Who else have we got that's far enough inside?"

"Grigor Bedrossian."

"Shiv." I stood and greeted the man who'd just joined us. "How's Pimm?"

"I'll be fine, you stupid fucking asshole."

Shiv stepped aside, and Pimm walked toward me and reached out his hand.

"You armed?"

"Shake my hand, ya wanker."

I did. "I'm sorry."

"Forgiven."

"Why?"

"Gunner, thank the man for accepting your bloody apology," said Shiv. "We have an op to finish."

"What do you want to know about Bedrossian?" Pimm asked.

"Nothing," answered Razor. "I want to track Svetlana Ivashov's whereabouts for the last twenty years."

"Bedrossian would be the man."

"Is your cover blown?" I asked.

"What cover? He knows I'm MI6. So is he, actually. At one point anyway. When his uncle became president, he immediately appointed Grigor as ambassador to the UK. Now that the pres needs more help from you Yanks, he sent him to DC."

"Get me everything you can on Svetlana and Topor Evasov," Razor said to Pimm.

"Svetlana's brother?"

"What?" Razor and I gasped simultaneously.

"I'm beginning to think we don't work together on jack shit," I shot at Shiv.

"He's actually her stepbrother. Different fathers," added Pimm.

I peeked my head out of the room we were in but didn't see Raketa. "Excuse me, gentlemen."

I found her sitting outside, looking up at the sky. "Hey, Rocket Girl."

"Hi," she answered, nuzzling into me when I sat next to her.

"How'd your chat with Ava go?"

"It was fine. You were right."

"She didn't ask questions."

"None at all."

"Good."

"What have you been doing?"

I told her that I'd asked Razor what he knew about Topor Evasov. "What about you? What's his background?"

"I don't know much of anything."

"He's your uncle."

Raketa turned her head. "Explain."

I reiterated the conversation Razor and I'd had with Shiv and Pimm.

"Wow," she said, looking up at the sky again and shaking her head. "He hates me so much."

"Maybe he doesn't."

"You should've seen him."

"Who else saw him?"

"What do you mean?"

"Surveillance, right?"

Raketa nodded.

"How do you think it would've gone down if Petrov thought Topor's behavior to you was too...familiar? Did he ever hurt you?"

"Not really. He used to get rough and drag me by my arm, but nothing worse than that."

The front door opened, and Shiv came outside.

"I'm sorry to interrupt, but we need to wrap things up so you can leave."

"Come on," I said to Raketa, taking her hand in mine.

The K19 team had reassembled in the main room of Doc and Merrigan's house. All eyes were on Shiv and me when we came inside.

"The meeting with UR has been accelerated," Doc told us.

"Meaning what?" I asked.

"It's going down in about thirty minutes."

"How?"

"They're coming here," Doc answered.

"Have you lost your mind?" I couldn't believe Doc would allow UR anywhere near his compound, let alone his wife and baby.

"They aren't coming to the house. You, Shiv, and McTiernan are meeting them at San Ysidro Ranch. We've made arrangements for a cottage. You'll have plenty of cover."

"Why the change?" asked Shiv.

"There's new intel on Petrov's twenty."

My head was about to explode. "Where is he, Doc?"

"On the move. It appears he's heading south."

"Where'd the intel come from?"

"Ambassador Bedrossian," answered Pimm.

I nodded and then looked at Raketa. She had no visible reaction to anything that had been said, and that was her training kicking in. It occurred to me that the only times she had a visceral reaction, was when we were alone.

"Are you ready?" I asked McTiernan.

"Yes."

The answer was simple, and I didn't need more than that.

"Who's staying, who's going?" I asked Doc, who rattled off each of the teams. Half of the K19 team would stay put with Raketa, Doc, Merrigan, and Quinn along with Ava, her sister, and mother. The rest were going with me and Shiv.

"When this deal is done, we're leaving Doc and Merrigan alone for a long while," I said to the group.

"Roger that," said Razor.

For the most part, Razor kept his facial reactions to a minimum, but he had two tells. One, when he was lying. That one his wife had recognized early on. The second was when he was stressed. Tonight his anxiety level was through the roof, and I understood why. In fact, I'd guess Doc and Shiv were equally stressed. To them, this was personal; to the rest, it was a mission.

42

Zary

There was a mental routine I implemented when the stress of whatever situation I was in threatened to undermine my focus.

Regardless of whether I stayed here or went with the team meeting with United Russia, I was in grave danger. Until the deal was made—if it was made—UR could mount a full-bore attack and kill not just me, but anyone around me. I knew this from experience.

Gunner was at an equal level of risk. There was no question that United Russia knew exactly how important he was to me, and would use that as a means to punish me for what I'd done when I left their employ.

"Come with me," Merrigan said, leading me upstairs. "I think I have a good idea of your mental state presently, and I'd like to offer some perspective."

I nodded while I waited for Merrigan to close the door to the room we were in.

"If anyone from K19, MI6, or the agency weren't completely confident that this deal was viable, this meeting wouldn't be taking place."

"I understand."

"If United Russia didn't see what's in it for them, it wouldn't be taking place either, and they certainly wouldn't have agreed to move it up forty-eight hours."

Unless they were planning an annihilation. I recognized that their doing so would mean the equivalent of World War III. Taking out that number of operatives with connections to both the CIA and MI6 would spell political and financial ruin for UR. Even China wouldn't step in to help them if they put themselves in that position.

Without money and support from the members of the United Nations Security Council, UR would be ripe for a coup. It didn't matter how many friends their current leader had inside his homeland; no world power could continue as such without allies.

"I can see you're lost in thought, adding to my list of considerations."

I nodded. "It's logical they would not jeopardize the Russian Federation's position in the UN or among its members."

"Exactly," said Merrigan. "You also know that UR's enemies within the federation are many."

I nodded a second time. The United States was also often a hotbed of political turmoil, but here, differences were settled by way of elections. There was no shortage of hatred between political parties, but in the nation's almost two-hundred-and-fifty-year history, there'd never been a governmental overthrow, and the odds of one ever happening were astronomically low.

"In other words, they aren't bloody stupid."

I heard a knock at the door.

"Come in," said Merrigan.

"I'm sorry to interrupt, but we're heading out," said Gunner, his eyes focused solely on mine.

"I'll give you a minute." Merrigan closed the door behind her.

"I love you, Zary," he said, cupping my cheek with his palm.

"I love you, Gunner. Be careful," I whispered.

"Always."

I clung to him in a way I'd never done with anyone in my life.

"This is a big piece of the puzzle, Raketa, and to be honest, as much as I initially questioned Doc's decision, I know now that I wouldn't have accepted not being a part of this meeting. I wouldn't have trusted anyone else to make sure it got done. I know Shiv feels the same way."

"Thank you."

"I don't want your thanks. It's you and me from here on out. We're together, and we're going to stay that way for the rest of our very long lives. I'd say we're a team, but we're so much more than that."

When Gunner said we were so much more than a team before he left, I'd almost confessed my plan and begged him to let me come with him. Knowing he'd refuse and then ask one of the K19 partners to keep an eye on me, I stayed silent.

I'd studied the security setup of Doc's compound, including how vehicles were able to leave through the gate without a code being entered.

Earlier, I'd watched Razor set his car key on the counter, near his laptop, before going upstairs to check on Ava. It hadn't taken much to slip it into my pocket. If he'd noticed it was gone, I'd have simply slipped it back out somewhere else where it would be easy for him to find. He hadn't noticed, though.

No one commented when I said I was going outside for a few minutes, and evidently, no one noticed Razor's car start up or pull out of the gate.

According to my GPS, the ranch where Doc had said the meeting was taking place was only a few miles away. I'd have to hide the car, figure out a place where I could surveil what cottage they were meeting in, and then wait to make my move.

I didn't plan to act unless it became warranted, and Gunner was in danger.

I parked behind a storage building and was creeping through the heavy growth of trees and bushes when I saw several cars, including one that I recognized as belonging to K19.

Before I could take another step, I saw something else that turned my blood to ice.

Petrov was also getting out of a different vehicle, one that had been parked farther away, with my mother held firmly in his grasp.

Someone must've tipped him off about the meeting, and he planned to use my mother as either a shield or a bargaining chip. Had they been discussing the change in the location prior to Doc removing the tracking device from my body? I didn't think so, which meant he had to have someone on the inside, reporting to him. Maybe Gunner's instincts about Pimm had been right after all.

I could follow, maybe even kill Petrov before he had a chance to act, but that meant my shot had to be dead-on. It had been years since I'd executed a nighttime kill without the assistance of an NVD.

I felt the gun pressed against my temple at the same time I heard a familiar voice say, "Don't make a sound or a move."

Topor. Once again he'd caught me off guard. Instead of assessing my surroundings, I'd only been focused on Petrov and my mother.

"Keep quiet and your mother might live. Make a sound and she'll be dead instantaneously."

In the next few seconds, all hell broke loose outside the back of the cottage. I watched in horror as Gunner and Shiv came out and found themselves face-to-face with Petrov, who pressed his gun into my mother's temple the same way Topor's was still pressed against mine. My worst nightmare had come true. My mother and I would die tonight, and there was nothing I could do to stop it from happening.

43

Gunner

Something was off. I could feel it in my bones. I studied McTiernan as he outlined the deal we'd brought to the Russians, kept my eye on Shiv and Striker, and watched the three other men from United Russia who were with us in the dimly lit room.

If Razor were here, it would take one look between us for him to know my hackles were raised, and vice versa. Neither Shiv nor Striker had made eye contact with me at all.

Every man in the room, with the exception of McTiernan and his UR counterpart, had their hands on their guns—me included. All things being equal, neither organization could take the other out…unless one of us had less backup posted outside. K19 had four— Monk, Onyx, Alegria, and Dutch. United Russia had agreed to the same number, but it was anyone's guess as to whether they stuck to the deal or not.

"Wait. This wasn't part of our agreement," I heard McTiernan say. The man turned around and looked between Shiv and me.

Shiv approached while I kept watch.

"The terms cannot be changed at this juncture," Shiv snapped, standing and glaring at the Russian negotiator whose only response was a smug look I wanted to rip off his face.

"What's changed?" I asked Shiv.

"They've added Petrov."

"He was already part of it."

"We have to deliver him to them instead of the other way around."

The idea didn't exactly bother me, but the fact that UR was changing things now pissed me off as much as it did Shiv.

"Dead or alive?" I asked.

Shiv looked back down at the document. "Either."

Killing Petrov would be my pleasure, but I wanted the deal done now anyway.

As I contemplated our next move, I saw a shadowed figure right outside the window. It appeared that whoever it was, wasn't alone.

"*Code black,*" I barked, and every light in the place immediately went out. It was a different meaning for a commonly used code that Striker, Shiv, and I had agreed to prior to the start of the meeting. "We have company, gentlemen," I whispered in the now-silent room.

"Who?" asked Shiv.

"I'm almost positive it's Petrov, and if so, he just made finalizing this agreement far easier."

Shiv, me, and two of the Russians slipped on night-vision devices. Shiver and I crept to the back door while the Russians went out the front.

"We've got company," I whispered into my mic.

The fact that he wasn't wearing an NVD didn't seem to thwart Petrov at all. There was enough light from the moon and the other cottages that he could see exactly who and what he was up against.

I studied him as he contemplated his next move. There was a flash of confusion on Petrov's face. It was likely he'd anticipated walking in on a different scenario. But what?

He held a woman I guessed was Raketa's mother at gunpoint, but otherwise, it appeared he'd arrived without backup.

"Drop the gun, Makar," I heard Shiv shout. "You're vastly outnumbered."

We all heard the sound of movement from behind him. I leveled my weapon in the direction of the noise at the same time as I watched Petrov fire a second gun into the dark. Immediately after which, we heard the sound of someone hitting the ground.

"You see, being outnumbered will do nothing to deter me. I'm here for my daughters."

"Which daughters are those?" I taunted.

"You well know, don't you? Zaryana, my oldest, and my beloved twin girls, Ava and Aine."

"They aren't here," Shiv shouted. "It seems whomever you've got on the inside set you up for an ambush."

"*Bullshit.* I know my daughters are here. You have two choices. Hand them over, or Zaryana's precious mother dies."

"Shiver is telling the truth," I said, taking a step toward him. "Your three daughters are in a safe place far away from here. Want proof?" When I made a move for my phone, Petrov pressed the gun more firmly against the trembling woman's temple and shielded himself with her body.

"*Devochka moya,*" I heard her softly cry when I eased another step forward.

44

Zary

Topor held a second gun to my back and pushed me in the direction of the woods. I could no longer see what was happening, but I heard Petrov offer my mother in exchange for me, Ava, and Aine.

"Let her go, Petrov, and you live," I heard Gunner respond. "You have ten seconds until I shoot." He started counting backwards from ten.

"Move," grunted Topor, pushing me to walk faster. At the same time, Topor shoved me into the car, I heard Gunner yell for everyone to stand down.

"No!" I cried when I heard a single gunshot, followed by the sound of one set of footsteps, growing fainter as whoever it was ran into the forest.

"Shut up, you stupid girl," Topor seethed.

What had happened? Had Petrov shot my mother? Were his footsteps the ones I heard running away? If so, why didn't I hear more shots, or more footsteps running after him?

45

Gunner

"I'm leaving, but if you come after me, she still dies." Petrov held up a device that was hard to see in the dark.

"Stand down," I yelled when Petrov shoved Svetlana away from him.

When Shiver fired, I grabbed his arm, diverting the shot into the trees.

"What the fuck?" Shiv shouted, taking off toward the woods.

I grabbed him again, this time winding my arm around Shiv's neck. *"Let him go."*

"Why?"

"She's wired." I showed him where a device was wrapped around Svetlana's midsection. "We have to diffuse it."

"You fucking diffuse it; I'm going after Petrov," Shiv yelled, trying to wrench free of my chokehold.

"You can't. You heard him. He'll kill her and maybe us along with her."

"I *have* to kill him, Gunner. I have to. How can you not understand?"

"I do, Shiv, but there's something you need to know."

"Fuck off, Gunner. Let go of me." Shiv tugged at my arm.

"Raketa refused to hand over Kuznetsov, even to save her own life," I said, releasing him.

"If we don't get Petrov, UR will kill both of them."

"Shiv!" I shouted as the man started walking toward the forest. *"Would Kuznetsov want you to give up Raketa's mother?"*

I watched the pain of acceptance wash over Shiver's face. We both knew, for now, going after Petrov wasn't an option. First, we had to make sure Svetlana was safe.

"We'll get him, Shiv. I promise. But we have to do this first."

He nodded, and I motioned for the rest of the team to come closer.

"We believe this is an explosive device that Petrov is able to detonate remotely."

Onyx stepped forward. "Let me have a look," he said.

Shiv turned to me, and I nodded. "He's the best we've got."

I looked for the UR team and found them seemingly immobilized by the scene that had played out in front of them. What they needed was someone like Raketa to kick their asses into shape. But she wasn't theirs anymore. She was mine, and I couldn't wait to get back to Doc's and hold her in my arms.

I remembered the shot Petrov fired. "Who's missing?" I asked. "Check with the Russians too."

"Alegria," said Dutch.

"Go find her," I told him, praying she wasn't dead, but doubting she could be alive. How close had she been when Petrov got the one shot off that had resulted in someone dropping to the ground? It had to have been very close for him to have hit her.

46

Zary

I didn't speak as the vehicle barreled out of the ranch's parking lot. I had no idea where we were going, but did it matter? Soon we'd meet up with Petrov, who would threaten my life in exchange for me handing over whatever money he'd put in my name. Once I had, he'd kill me anyway.

The familiar sounds of a gun being prepared to be fired didn't faze me. How could it be this easy for me to accept my own mortality? Had I been preparing myself for it all my life?

I didn't believe in heaven or hell, and there wasn't much I regretted. Not being able to save my mother's life, for she was surely dead by now, and Gunner. Always Gunner.

How long had I loved him? More than ten years, and they'd all been wasted. If I'd told him that first night, when I spared his life, that I wanted to leave United Russia, would he have taken me with him? Would he have offered me his asylum in exchange for the shot I'd fired into the ground? I'd never know.

At least I'd been able to tell him how I felt and hear that he loved me too. That knowledge would sustain me through whatever happened next. If Petrov was capable of mercy, maybe he'd let Topor kill me quickly.

The vehicle came to a stop, and Topor killed the engine. It hadn't taken long for us to arrive at the place where I'd breathe my last breath. I squared my shoulders and raised my chin. I wasn't a coward, even in the face of death.

I felt Topor fumbling with the blindfold. When I opened my eyes, I saw my gun in his hand.

"Here," he said, motioning for me to take it.

"Why?"

"In the next few minutes, either you or I are going to kill Petrov."

The intel had been correct. "You're my uncle."

Topor nodded as he prepped a second gun. "And we're about to kill your father."

"He's not my father. He's the devil."

Topor nodded again. "Let's go."

Petrov's breathing was labored as Topor and I approached him.

"Ah, not in a protected location after all, Zaryana," he said to me with an evil grin. "Good work, Topor."

I'd known, without my uncle saying it, that the gun he held pressed against my back was only for show. It would get us close enough to Petrov for one of us to kill him.

I slowly pulled the 9mm Luger semi-automatic pistol from my back pocket. At the same time, a car's headlights illuminated the scene, and I watched as Topor turned his gun from me to Petrov.

Petrov's eyes widened in the split second when he realized what was about to happen. *"What the f—"*

Both shots fired hit the frontal lobe of his head, spattering brain matter in the air as Makar Petrov's body hit the ground with an anti-climactic thud. Which shot had killed him? It didn't matter. Both my uncle and I could hold our retribution to the evil bastard close.

47

Gunner

"It was an amateur job. Something someone could have learned how to do from the internet," Onyx told us as he tossed the explosive device's components to the side after diffusing it in under a minute.

"She's alive," Dutch yelled, carrying Alegria in his arms.

"I've already called for a bus," shouted Striker.

"Get another one on the way," I said, holding Svetlana's limp body in my arms. She was alive, although she'd likely been drugged enough to keep her pliable to Petrov's plan, but not enough that she'd be unconscious, until now.

Striker scrubbed his face with his hand. "Roger that, Gunner, but we need to talk. Immediately. You too, Shiv."

"What's going on?" Shiv asked.

"The Russians have taken the entire deal off the table."

"Why?"

"Because you let Petrov go."

"Jesus fucking Christ. You've got to be shitting me?" We'd chosen to save a woman's life and diffuse a bomb that could've killed everyone in her proximity if it had been detonated. That was very different than letting Petrov go.

"This isn't over," I announced to all those assembled. "Onyx, you ride the bus with Alegria." If Alegria hadn't been injured herself, she'd be the one riding with Svetlana. That left Striker, Dutch, and Monk. Striker had to help us get this deal back on the table, and Monk had communication…issues.

"Dutch, you ride with Svetlana." Another thing occurred to me. "Do you speak Azeri?"

Dutch shook his head.

"Russian? Armenian?"

"Negative."

"Contact Pimm and have him meet you at the hospital." Raketa's mother would need someone who could explain what had happened to her, and reassure her of her safety while, at the same time, figure out if she knew where Petrov might have gone.

I looked over at Shiv, who was studying his phone. His eyes met mine, and I didn't like what I saw in them.

"Raketa?" I asked, not knowing why, other than the feeling of dread that settled in my stomach.

Shiv nodded. "I'm afraid Petrov may have her."

"How in the hell?"

"She left Doc's compound a half hour ago."

"And you know this how?"

"You know the answer, Gunner. We need to go find her before Petrov has a chance to kill her."

Our vehicle came to a stop close enough that I could see Raketa and Topor turn their guns on Petrov, shoot, and kill him while Shiver and I ran toward them.

I heard someone screaming her name, and realized when she turned and looked at me that the voice I heard was my own.

She threw her gun to the ground and bolted in my direction. When our bodies collided, I lifted her into my arms, and she wrapped her legs around me.

"He's dead," she repeated as I stroked her hair.

I reached into my pocket with my free hand, pulled out a phone, and took a photo of Petrov's lifeless body.

Finish it, the text read that accompanied the photo I sent.

Roger that, answered Striker.

Epilogue

Gunner

Zary lay naked in my arms in front of the fireplace, the only sound coming from the crackling wood and the waves hitting the shore of the beach.

Twenty-four hours ago, we'd left Montecito and drove to my house in Cambria. Razor may have done the same with Ava, but I didn't know or care.

At some point, there'd be a hotwash of the deal that had been finalized with United Russia, as well as the part of the op that had resulted in Petrov's death. I didn't care about that either.

Within minutes of arriving at my beach house, my Rocket Girl and I had torn off our clothes and made love—the first of many times. The need for condoms crossed my mind, but I let it go. If Zary got pregnant, it would simply mean we'd be one step closer to building a family.

Neither of us had spoken much during the two-hour drive other than to profess our love again.

Like I'd left Paps behind after I'd killed Lena, Zary told me she was letting Raketa go. She'd always be my Rocket Girl, but she'd never again use the name under which she'd been a Russian assassin.

She was still as badass as ever and would be welcome to join the K19 team if that was what she wanted. But if she wanted to retire, I'd join her.

I closed my eyes, remembering how her steely facade had faded in my arms last night as I carried her away from Petrov's corpse. Everyone else could buy the image of the cold, hard killer that she projected to the world. Only I knew that, underneath, she was as vulnerable and sensitive as I was.

I felt the chill on her flesh, took her in my arms, and carried her upstairs to the bed that was no longer mine. For the rest of our lives, every bed we slept in would be ours—no matter where it was housed.

My phone vibrated several times before I picked it up. "This better be about a fucking nuclear holocaust," I told the caller. "Nothing else could warrant your intrusion."

Shiver laughed. "This will be quick. I wanted to give you an update on Svetlana."

I walked out of the bedroom and closed the door so I didn't wake the woman sound asleep in our bed.

"Right," I answered, knowing that the subject of her mother's well-being would be on par with World War III for Zary. "How is she?"

"She latched on to Pimm and wouldn't let go until Topor showed up. They're keeping her overnight for observation, but you and Raketa can come get her in the morning. Fair warning that you may have to let Topor accompany her."

"How did his interrogation go?"

"It was brief, but informative. He's willing to cooperate with whatever we need."

"Will he name names?"

"Yes, that's part of his deal."

"How's Alegria?"

"Critical, but stable. Mantis hasn't left her side."

"Why?" There was no need for security any longer as far as I knew.

Shiver laughed a second time. "Are you really saying you don't know?"

"Know what?"

Shiver was still laughing. "Mantis and Alegria."

"Are you saying they're together?"

"On and off for years," said Shiv.

It was one more thing I hadn't been aware of, just like I hadn't known anything about Shiv and Kuznetsov. A few days ago, my not knowing would've bothered me. Now I didn't care if I ever got a briefing again, about anything.

"Anything else *vital* I need to know? And by that, I mean something that pertains only to Zary and me."

"Not a thing," answered Shiv. "But, *Zary?*"

The man's chuckling was starting to piss me off.

"Later, asshole," I said, disconnecting the call.

From inside the bedroom, I heard the sweet voice of my woman, calling my name.

"Coming, sweetheart," I answered, climbing back into bed.

"Who was that?"

"Shiver. We'll be able to bring your mother home tomorrow."

"Oh. Um…where?"

"Wherever we are, Zary, she'll be with us."

She smiled. "I'd like to take her to your island."

"*Our* island, baby.

Keep reading for a sneak peek at
the first book in Heather Slade's
Royal Agents of MI6 Series,
Make Me Shiver

An MI6 agent falling for the wrong woman.
A Russian assassin with secrets to hide.
And the passion that defies the rules...

THE DUKE

My team. My family. My allegiance. As a duke, the boundaries and loyalties are clear. I may be the Marquess of Wells with a stoic father on his deathbed, but I have desires and needs that break those boundaries. Falling for an assassin may be an issue. But I haven't faced a problem yet that I can't solve—other than assembling a crib.

THE ASSASSIN

Secrets. Lies. Deception. As a Russian assassin, I'm riddled with it all. Now, with a ten-million-dollar bounty on my head, there's no way I can get out alive. But the irresistible and incorrigible duke thinks otherwise. He wants me in his life, in his arms, and in his bed. But when he discovers my secret, can he ever forgive me?

1

Shiver

"Thornton, are you listening?"

I turned away from the window where I'd been looking out at the dormant gardens of Whittaker Abbey. The land had been handed down, heir to heir, since 1547 when the former Cistern abbey was taken over by Henry VIII. Shortly afterward, the estate was given to John Whittaker as a gift from the king for his service.

As a boy, I'd explored every acre of the forested estate and its gardens, knowing that one day, the care and maintenance of the land would be my responsibility. It had seemed a long way off then—not until I was an old man, when my father, the fourteenth Duke, passed away.

Until then, I would remain the Marquess of Wells and, more importantly to me, a high-ranking agent in the United Kingdom's Secret Intelligence Service, also known as Military Intelligence Section 6, or MI6.

"I beg your pardon, Duchess," I answered, looking at my mother, the woman who had been the guiding force of our family in the months since my father had suffered a debilitating stroke.

"Come, sit with me," she said, holding her hand out to me. "Tell me what's troubling you."

I sat, but had no intention of confiding in her. I also had no intention of lying, so chose not to say anything.

"Have you seen your father this morning?" she asked.

"I read the news to him."

My mother patted my hand. "You know how much he likes to catch up over his morning tea."

I doubted my father had heard a word I read, and he'd certainly not had any tea, but as the doctors had told us, the important thing was that the family spent time with him and conversed whether the duke was able to respond or not.

"There's more," she murmured.

"What's that?"

"Something is on your mind, Thornton, and whatever it is, its weight is heavy."

Even if I wanted to discuss it with my mother, I wouldn't know where to begin.

"It's a woman."

I leaned closer. "It's nothing," I said softly. "Let it be, Duchess."

"For now," she said, standing and leaning down to kiss my cheek. "I'll check on your father."

I nodded and stood too, walking back over to the window.

It had been over a month since United Russia lifted the ten-million-dollar bounty they had on Orina "Losha" Kuznetsov's head, and yet I had no idea where she was and why she insisted on staying so far underground that no one could find her.

I'd called in every favor—and there had been many—but so far, I didn't have a single lead as to where the bloody woman was hiding.

Keep reading for a sneak peek at the next
book in Heather Slade's
K19 Security Solutions Team One Series,
Mistletoe's Magic

**More is at stake than a
holiday surprise or two…**

The K19 Security Solutions team is typically ready to serve and protect at any given time. But the holidays call for even more vigilance and protection—from each other. As families navigate through Thanksgiving and Christmas, more conflicts arise. Just as Zary and Gunner discover a Christmas miracle, Ava and Razor have a secret of their own.

Can the men and woman of K19 Security Solutions make it to the New Year without destroying the magic of the holidays or will the season bring more than they bargained for?

1

—Mantis—

Compared to some of the places I'd been forced to sleep during my career, the hospital recliner was damn comfortable.

I shifted to my left side, hoping it would relieve some of the pressure on the right, where a bullet had struck my hip, requiring pelvic reconstruction surgery. The good news was, it hadn't been life threatening and none of my organs had been compromised. The arthritic pain, however, was unrelenting.

I looked over at the woman lying in the hospital bed, hoping her injuries wouldn't result in a similar life of pain. No one deserved to live with the kind I had to, but Alegria deserved it less than anyone I'd ever known.

We'd met at the United States Air Force Academy when I was a senior and she was an international student one year behind me. I remembered the day our Air Officer Commanding, AOC, introduced Manon "Alegria" Mondreau to the squadron. She was the most beautiful woman I'd ever seen. Still was.

Her ebony-black hair was pulled back into the tight bun required by Air Force regulations, highlighting her mesmerizing, almond-shaped, gray-blue eyes.

How many times had I kissed her pouty, cherry-colored lips and ran my hands over her seductively sculpted nubile body? Hundreds.

"Any change?" asked Dutch, who'd known both Manon and me since those early days when we were all cadets, anxious to begin pilot training and get on with our careers.

I shook my head. "Nothing."

"Why don't you take a break? I can sit with her for the next couple of hours."

"Thanks, but I'll stick around."

"Mantis—"

I raised my hand. "I have to be here, Dutch. Don't fight me on this."

My friend nodded and sat in one of the other recliners the hospital staff had agreed to bring into the room.

"She's out of intensive care. That's a good sign, right?" Dutch asked.

It was, but they still had no idea whether the damage to Manon's spinal cord would have lasting effects.

"What happened between you two? Last I heard, you were thinking about proposing."

As Dutch well knew, I'd taken an assignment. One she didn't want me to.

***

"You volunteer more than anyone else. Why?"

"It's my duty, Manon. It's what I signed up for."

"It's no longer a duty. You retired. We agreed—"

"No. Stop right there. We didn't agree to anything. You demanded I quit, and I refused. That's the way it went down."

She shook her head and stormed off. There'd been a time I would've gone after her, but no more. She'd spent just as much time stateside as she had in France, yet she still lived by her native country's work ethic. Or lack of it.

It wasn't that she didn't like to work; Manon was just able to compartmentalize better than I was. She could say no to assignments without thinking twice. I couldn't remember ever turning one down.

A few minutes later, she was back. "If you go, we're finished."

"I won't choose you over my country, Manon."

***

What had made matters worse, the assignment required me to go deep undercover, and during that time, no one knew whether I was dead or alive, and if I was still breathing, when I might resurface.

I had come back, finally, but Manon was steadfast in her refusal to forgive me for what she considered a betrayal.

I tried to get in touch with her when I first returned, but she'd refused to answer my calls. I knew from Doc that she was still on the K19 team, but the boss hadn't encouraged me to continue pursuing her.

"Hold back for now," he'd advised. "She knows you're back. Let her come to you."

I'd questioned Doc's advice, but in the end, abided by it. What choice did I have? She refused to respond to my calls, texts, or emails.

"Is she with someone else?" I'd asked.

"Not that I'm aware of. However, Mantis, the personal lives of K19 team members are none of my business."

I almost laughed at Doc's proclamation, given the man had his nose in everyone else's business about as much as my best friend, Dutch, did.

I stood and walked over to the bed when Manon groaned. I stroked her forehead, willing her to open her eyes and look at me.

"Mon coeur," I whispered when she did.

"Où suis-je?"

"L'hôpital." I was reaching the limit of words I knew in French, besides the obvious ones everyone knew. "You were shot."

"Petrov?"

I nodded.

"Surgery?"

"Yes."

She turned her head and looked away from me, noticing for the first time that Dutch was in the room. She reached out her hand for him in the way I would've expected her to reach for me.

I met Dutch's eyes when he stood, and in them, I saw sadness and guilt.

The man who'd been my best friend for twenty years took his time walking the three or four steps it would take him to get to the opposite side of the bed.

I felt my throat close up as my precious Manon clung to Dutch's hand. I realized then that I was the interloper in the room, not Dutch. Not the man who, only minutes before, had asked what happened between she and I.

I turned and walked out of the room, cursing myself for being such a fool.

About the Author

USA Today and Amazon Top 15 Bestselling Author Heather Slade writes shamelessly sexy, edge-of-your seat romantic suspense.

She gave herself the gift of writing a book for her own birthday one year. Forty-plus books later (and counting), she's having the time of her life.

The women Slade writes are self-confident, strong, with wills of their own, and hearts as big as the Colorado sky. The men are sublimely sexy, seductive alphas who rise to the challenge of capturing the sweet soul of a woman whose heart they'll hold in the palm of their hand forever. Add in a couple of neck-snapping twists and turns, a page-turning mystery, and a swoon-worthy HEA, and you'll be holding one of her books in your hands.

She loves to hear from my readers. You can contact her at heather@heatherslade.com

To keep up with her latest news and releases, please visit her website at www.heatherslade.com to sign up for her newsletter.

MORE FROM AUTHOR HEATHER SLADE

BUTLER RANCH
Kade's Worth
Brodie's Promise
Maddox's Truce
Naughton's Secret
Mercer's Vow
Kade's Return
Butler Ranch Christmas

WICKED WINEMAKERS
FIRST LABEL
Brix's Bid
Ridge's Release
Press' Passion
Zin's Sins
Tryst's Temptation

WICKED WINEMAKERS
SECOND LABEL
Beau's Beloved
Coming Soon:
Cru's Crush
Bones' Bliss
Snapper's Seduction
Kick's Kiss

ROARING FORK RANCH
Coming Soon:
Roaring Fork Wrangler
Roaring Fork Roughstock
Roaring Fork Rockstar
Roaring Fork Rooker
Roaring Fork Bridger

THE ROYAL AGENTS
OF MI6
Make Me Shiver
Drive Me Wilder
Feel My Pinch
Chase My Shadow
Find My Angel

K19 SECURITY
SOLUTIONS TEAM ONE
Razor's Edge
Gunner's Redemption
Mistletoe's Magic
Mantis' Desire
Dutch's Salvation

K19 SECURITY
SOLUTIONS TEAM TWO
Striker's Choice
Monk's Fire
Halo's Oath
Tackle's Honor
Onyx's Awakening

K19 SHADOW OPERATIONS
TEAM ONE
Code Name: Ranger
Code Name: Diesel
Code Name: Wasp
Code Name: Cowboy
Code Name: Mayhem

K19 ALLIED INTELLIGENCE
TEAM ONE
Code Name: Ares
Code Name: Cayman
Code Name: Poseidon
Code Name: Zeppelin
Code Name: Magnet

K19 ALLIED INTELLIGENCE
TEAM TWO
Coming Soon:
Code Name: Puck
Code Name: Michelangelo
Code Name: Typhon
Code Name: Hornet
Code Name: Reaper

PROTECTORS
UNDERCOVER
Undercover Agent
Undercover Emissary
Coming Soon:
Undercover Savior
Undercover Infidel
Undercover Assassin

THE INVINCIBLES
TEAM ONE
Decked
Edged
Grinded
Riled
Smoked

THE INVINCIBLES
TEAM TWO
Bucked
Irished
Sainted
Hammered
Ripped

THE UNSTOPPABLES
TEAM ONE
Furied
Married

COWBOYS OF
CRESTED BUTTE
A Cowboy Falls
A Cowboy's Dance
A Cowboy's Kiss
A Cowboy Stays
A Cowboy Wins